A LOT LESS LIKE ME,
A LOT LESS OF ME

A LOT LESS LIKE ME, A LOT LESS OF ME

SUPARNA JAIN

PARTRIDGE

To order additional copies of this book, contact
Partridge India
000 800 10062 62
orders.india@partridgepublishing.com

www.partridgepublishing.com/india

Dedicated to my brother Shubham Jain
who always tells me one thing
"Tu jaanti nahi hai tu kya cheez hai"

ACKNOWLEDGEMENT

I cannot thank the three most important people in my life, enough for supporting me through the entire process of writing this book. Mom for constantly reminding me that I need to write and for the emotional support.

Dad for being the silent motivation and the back bone of my life.

Bhai for pulling me up every time I thought of giving up.

Mamu, Avinder Singh for always encouraging me to chase my dreams and my cousins for their support.

And now the soul of this book, Sonika and Reshma. For their reading sessions and detailed feedbacks. Thanks guys. I owe you big time.

Saif for convincing me to take up this project.

A special mention to Divya Ma'am, as I would not be writing this book had she not been there. I love you ma'am.

Thank you Prerna and Archana ma'am for the proof reading sessions.

Thank you Sunila ma'am for having faith in me since I was 7 and Kamini ma'am for making me realise who I was.

My alma mater Convent of Jesus and Marry and St. Bede's College Shimla.

Manipal University for giving direction to my wings and Amity University for polishing them.

Thank You everyone, because this book would not have been possible without you guys.

CHAPTER 1

6 a.m. in the morning and I am getting ready for my first day at Rawat sir's math's tuition classes. Well it was just a start towards preparing better for my class 12 board exams and I was happy about it that I was going to a centre where I would learn a lot and grow. Dad came along with me to drop me to the institute as early mornings could be really scary. A morning walk with dad for the first time and that too on his birthday, I was super excited. Moreover the walk in the hills is such bliss. It was heavenly to walk down the roads early morning watching the fresh dew drops on the leaves and the clouds rising up from the ground. Walking cutting past the clouds was a beautiful feeling altogether which one could experience only in a hill station and having grown up in such a town was nature's best gift to me.

No matter how old you grow, first day at any new place is always weird and uncomfortable. New people, different people everything is just random and unfamiliar. And same was the case with me. I did not know anyone there, but I guess that day I managed to pull through the class somehow.

The next day was better than the first one. I had started to familiarize myself, know and get comfortable with more people around. I had started to settle down and adjust to the environment. A few smiles exchanged and a hi! here and there made things even better and easygoing. I was the only one there from my school so it was a little difficult to make friends, people already knew each other and had groups right from school so it was a challenge to fit myself in there. But being the social butterfly I am, I guess I was managing things pretty well.

After class today this guy who usually sits on the last bench approached me. I could see him coming closer and I was getting nervous, but I tried to appear as calm as possible and pretending that I did not notice him coming my way.

"Hey, hi I'm Anikait Mahajan."

With a smile I greeted back and said "Hey, I'm Aditi."

"Science?" He asked.

"Nope, humanities" I smiled and answered.

"Aah, I guessed so" and we laughed together.

And just when I was wondering how he knew he said, "Don't worry, not stalking you, and didn't see you in any of the other classes for physics and chemistry so you know…"

I laughed and we walked along. And this is how I made my first friend at the Centre and felt may be a little more comfortable.

Two three days passed and things proceeded smoothly. Anikait would generally be with this group of boys from his school, but would definitely come up and say hi and eventually a few others from the group also started exchanging smiles. Except for this one guy. Oh my god what attitude he had. As if he was some Ranbir Kapoor. Well he was cute and all, and somewhat resembled him too, but what the hell, keep that attitude to yourself. I am in general very friendly with everyone around me, but if you have attitude problems I'm sorry deal with them on your own. And same was the case with him. I didn't even bother to try talking to him.

Almost a week later, we were all walking out of the centre when Anikait came from behind and said hi, we were having a word and just then, walked in Mr. Attitude. I had not even cared to find out his name till date so Anikait decided to introduce us. I'm sure he must have noticed that we don't talk to each other in fact we haven't even introduced ourselves, so he took the lead and introduced us.

"This is Akhil" said Anikait… and Mr. attitude stuck his hand out.

With the same attitude but with a smile, I too shook his hand and with equal attitude said "Hi, I'm Aditi."

Days passed by, the 'Hi' with which we initially took off grew into small conversations and within a week or two we had exchanged our phone numbers. Initially it started with texting just general forwards and jokes, but soon we started chatting about our own selves and then those random conversations started increasing. We spoke about our likes and dislikes, things we loved, things we hated and ya things we were scared of. Our past and how it was. He then told me about this girl he loved. Her name was Neha. They were together in school and had been together for 3 years but she cheated on him and left him. He expressed how much he loved her and how hurt and broken he was.

One evening we couldn't talk at the time we usually did, instead we chose to talk after dinner. He decided to just randomly scare me and said "Aditi there is someone at the window and I screamed." From here on till the end of our conversation that day he kept scaring me. It became a routine to talk to him in the evenings and when and how soon this routine turned into a habit we did not even realize. We dint get much time to interact otherwise. Because we were in two different schools and tuitions were scheduled in a manner such that we could not spend time together as we had to rush to school after that. So the only way we could interact was over the phone. But at that point of time, even that gave so much of happiness and satisfaction. Despite all the issues with not being able to meet up and spend time together, the phone conversations where enough to make us good friends soon. We had started understanding each other, sharing things and trusting each other.

It was November 24th, his birthday, by now we had become good friends and so I decided to give him a card and a chocolate. Didn't really want to give him a gift or something and give him a wrong signal. You know at this age giving a friend a gift for his birthday right away meant kind of expressing interest in him and so I didn't and decided to stick to a card and a chocolate. Well, nevertheless I guess that was a stepping stone for our relationship. Somehow this got us closer and what helped us was that school was over; no school meant no classes and more free time. All we had to do was, go for tuitions and do self-study at home. Which also on a brighter note meant we could spend some more time together after classes. Things changed. Life changed. For a change I was actually enjoying school life and lived carelessly.

The time we spent after classes was the best part of the day. We would walk through the kalibari road, down to the mall which was practically only a 5 minute walk but we would take ages to reach there and turn it into a never ending one. There were a few chat stalls on the way and being girls most of us from the group would want to stop by at one of them and have chat or our favourite golgappas. I too would be one of them, and most of the times I would land up listening to the same remark from him ;

"Keep having those round golgappas, no wonder you look just like them" and what followed was a sight which everyone treated themselves with. Our bags on the road, and me, running behind him to beat him. Thank god, no vehicles were allowed on that road or else either of us would have been run over by one of them for sure considering the way we ran. "Insane" the word is an understatement to describe how we behaved. But I guess it was these small moments which drew us closer to each other and we didn't realize when and how we became such good friends, those sms conversations turned into phone calls and those phone calls into feeling authoritative over each other.

An incident had happened with him about which I found out a little late. Akhil had gone out to celebrate his birthday with Anikait and a few other friends. And somehow all of this led to a lot of fights, arguments and misunderstandings which also led to a physical fight. He told me a few days later at the tuition centre when I asked him as to why he was so upset and off mood. Lately he was very quiet and not his mischievous self. That is when he told me what exactly had been bothering him all this while. I tried to calm him down and asked him to chuck the matter, but I guess the others involved had not yet let the matter pass by. It was Sunday and after class one of those people tried to pick up a fight, Akhil too started fighting back. I tried to ask him to stop fighting but he was not controllable and as a result I had to pull him back and take him away from there. At that moment all I wanted was to take him out of the fight and calm him down. He would have hurt himself and others, making things very ugly. It was hard but ya we managed. I was very scared. I had made him understand that there is no point fighting with these guys and sent him back home. But I was worried what if he came back and fought and hurt himself. Till the time he didn't get back to me and told me that he's home I was not at peace. And yes he had not gone back to fight or argue, instead he went back home.

This was the moment when I could say we had become best friends. Someone like him with serious attitude problems would never listen to anyone but this time he did listen to me. Why? Because even he took me as a close friend. By now our families were also aware of our growing friendship and bond. We would talk to them about each other and also we would be on the phone every evening, so it was expected that they would know about our relation.

His sister is really sweet, Sunidhi. A cute kid. 4 years younger to me but smart. Even she had started getting friendly with me and talking. Also at times complaining about how he misbehaved at home with uncle and aunty or how he does not study at home. She would tell me "Di he listens to you, so you should try talking to him about these things." Well she didn't have to say that, I anyways would have done that. But I understand her concern.

For me it has not always been important to be the kind of friend who would support you in anything you do, even if it is wrong. Instead I believe in pointing out mistakes when wrong and this is exactly what I did this time as well.

We kind of had a fixed timing now when either he would call or I would call and that would turn into our evening tea break, it was sometime around 5:30- 6:00 pm. It was like we knew that this call had to happen and so did our families and for this the phones were mostly kept free for us during that time. They knew it had been 5-6 hours since we have been away and it was time we spoke. More than just being friends' we also became a source of motivation for each other. Listening to each other became our duty and guiding not only our responsibility but more of a right. I made sure he studied and he made sure that I did the same too. Even though we were in the same race and fighting for our future there was no sense of competition whatsoever.

Then one fine day I picked up the topic of him misbehaving with his parents and that was one day I can say not only did I see a flip side of him but also the reason because of which I can, or rather he says 'You know me better than I know myself." That day onward our friendship took a different track, neither did he hide anything form me nor did I. The friendship only grew. There was no looking back. He began to concentrate more on his studies. He had also started avoiding Anikait and the group. I guess somewhere I was responsible for this distance between them, because I knew by moving away from them he would be able to set his life straight. I knew I was not doing the right thing, by asking him or in fact convincing him to maintain distance from them, but it was without any doubt the right thing for him at that point of time. It was the deciding time in our lives and I didn't want him to ruin it for the sake of friends who were with him just for his money and nothing else. They would study themselves and always misguide Akhil and distract him in their free time. On the other hand if he concentrated and studied he is very intelligent and can go really far but they just wouldn't let it happen and distract him every time he sat down to study. Things settled down a little now. He had also started studying and would indulge in useless activities comparatively less.

There were times when people around me discouraged me about myself and how at that point in time the only thing that mattered to me was studying. I would not hang out with friends for movies etc., but none of that affected me too much. The reason being my parents and him. Till the time they respected and supported my decisions I was okay with what anyone else had to say. I just didn't need anyone else around me. Preparations for exams raced faster. Well and just by the blink of an eye time passed by and board exams arrived.

We would meet on our way to school and the paper would be awesome or let's say I just felt more confident and stronger. Until the math's exam when something very unfortunate happened. I had a migraine attack while writing the paper and couldn't do well. I was shaken, disturbed and lost. Not knowing how to deal with it. I still had two more exams to go, but no motivation to write them. Akhil along with my parents encouraged me and gave me the strength to take the rest of my exams, but I could not put away the thought of one exam which was ruined. Well I somehow did write them but could not give my 100%. Exams got over which was a big relief but the bigger part was on its way, entrances where yet to begin. I was very demotivated to study. It was only his and my parent's support and encouragement that I took my exams. And soon Mumbai entrance result was out and I had got through and secured the 34th rank all over India. My dream of pursuing Journalism and Mass communication from the best college in the country had come true. Akhil too was happy for me. He had written many exams too for engineering but the results where yet to come.

We had gone to my grandma's place for a vacation. After the entire battle of exams and entrances a break was much needed. It was a very relaxed time with a light head. It was complete fun and fulfilling family time. One fine morning we found out that Salman khan was to visit the town and was going to cross our house too. I was super excited to see him and was getting ready and just then I got a call from Akhil. We started talking generally and I was telling him how excited I was to meet Salman khan. And suddenly cutting through what I was saying he said;

"Neha called up and wants to be back". I was surprised and shocked. The same girl who had left him for someone else and Akhil had cried so much for and then she didn't care to be with him and now suddenly she wants to come back. What does she want? This is not fair. You can't do this. It is painful for the other person.

"What does she have to say now?" I asked. I was very annoyed and was never too fond of her for the simple reason that she had hurt my best friend.

"She wants to get back. She says she has realised it was a mistake and that the guy was not what he seemed to be and now she wants us to be back again" said he.

"Oh" was all I could say at that point of time. I was taken aback. I could not feel anything or react to what he was saying. I was completely numb. He was talking and saying something, but what, I have no clue about that. In the meantime everyone started shouting, salman's here and they pulled me out as well, but I was in a complete state of trans, completely lost and could not move or say anything. After a while I called him back and he said;

"Yar, I'm not getting back with her." And there came a smile on my face, as if this was what I was waiting to listen to. When did Salman arrive and when he left and the other details were nowhere in my mind. All I could think off or focus on was Neha calling him and asking him to get back with her.

"Of course you can't go back to her, you're mine"

I said to him. And he laughed. For a moment I started to think what did I just say? But then brushed the thought away. We then headed to Dharamshala with a few more cousin and I was high on god knows what and just smiling and happy.

Later I asked myself why I got the feeling of "You're mine when he said Neha wanted to get back? We're friends, best friends and he can have a girlfriend and I am free to have a boyfriend. So why this feeling of sharing him with someone made me feel like a volcanic eruption was happening within me. He someday has to be with someone, so why did just the thought of him being with someone else pinch me so much... why? And after a while I had an answer to it I was in LOVE. Yes, I had fallen in love with the same guy I didn't even want to talk to initially. I was in love with a boy I thought was someone full of attitude. I was in love with someone with whom I could be as stupid and weird I wanted to be, I was in love with my best friend.

It was a very new and a different feeling altogether. It took me a lot of time to get it to sink in to me, that I can fall in love. Something I use to dread and said I never will, and that too with Akhil. That is why they say, never say never. I had fallen in love with one of the most unreasonable, insensible, immature guy I knew. To round it up, someone I had never thought of falling in love with. A boy every mother would warn her daughter about. Someone who was not a picture perfect dream boy But I guess love just happens, no warning alarms, no preparation time, just happens. No matter how imperfect the other person might be it will just happen and change your world. It happened to me too, I always told myself I can never fall in love with someone like him but I guess I already had, with a boy totally opposite to my dream guy. But even then he just seemed perfect to me. It just felt right. It felt complete. But yes, it did take time for the feeling to settle down and for me to accept that I have fallen in love and that too with my best friend.

CHAPTER 2

They say the first love of your life stays with you forever and you can never forget it. I don't know about the whole forever jazz, but what I can surely say is that the feeling of loving someone is beautiful. Being in love is an ecstatic feeling. It takes you to a whole new world where everything except for love seems to be frozen It's pure and not affected or adulterated by any kind of past experiences, in short not bound by any kind of thoughts or hesitations. All you know is that you love the person, everything is crystal clear and the only thing that matters at that point in time is that you love that person and that's the end of it, what would be the outcome and the consequences of loving them does not bother you and is nowhere in your thoughts for that time and that time is the best time of your life.

I was going through such a phase in my life. Everything just seemed perfect. I felt beautiful for no reason at all, not that he appreciated me or anything of that sought, in fact he was not even aware of what was going on with me, but still there was a sense of completeness.

Our friendship was growing and getting stronger and I was cherishing every bit of it. Then came a day when we spoke about the kind of life partners we wanted and would want to settle down with at the end of the day. The definition of the kind of person I wanted now was completely different from what I have always thought off and I told him what kind of a person I had been waiting for. I'm sure after listening to the list he must have at least got a hint of what I felt for him.

Then came his turn to describe his ideal girl and my heart started skipping beats "What if I was nowhere close to what he wanted, what if he just says it outright." And then he started

"I want someone very beautiful"

1 point down, I was never very beautiful or sexy, and I skipped a beat again.

"I want someone loving"

Well I love you a lot; I thought to myself and smiled.

"I want someone who cares for me and my family"

Bingo, I can do that very well and then he said something that took me by surprise;

"I want someone who understands me just the way you do, to whom I don't have to explain what I want, how I feel and how I want to be treated, you just know it."

This gave me a different kind of kick and sent me to different world for a moment. I could not believe my ears.

Someone you love just said those words to you, what else would you want. We talked a lot that night. From songs to life, to friends and family and what happened next was a bit filmy, we decided to find partners for each other, and I whispered to myself "I have already found one for you."

We were happy with the way our friendship was growing and I was enjoying the feeling of my first love. Being in love with the person I have been the closest to after my family, being in love with someone who was a big part of my life and the best was being in love with my best friend.

Days were passing by and I was falling in love with him even more. Day's just seemed perfect. Life seemed beautiful. The feeling of loving someone was extremely fulfilling and my happiness knew no boundaries. I guess the happiness was not because I was in love but because the person I loved was with me. Yes, it was true that I had not told him about my feeling yet but sometimes a few things even when unsaid fill you with contentment.

By now people around me had started seeing the change in me, I was happier, joyful, dressed up all the time, took extra care of how I looked and ya blushed now and then. And when someone took his name, everything would just come to a halt and I would enter a completely new world. My days started with him and ended with him. I think it always was like that but the difference was that there was a different feeling of him being around now, a new outlook to the relationship altogether, it was different and special.

I had not told anyone about my feelings for him, not because I did not want to share it anyone. I wanted to shout it out loud and tell the world how much I loved him, but for now I just wanted to cherish the feeling. To be honest, somewhere down in my heart I was scared of losing him. Yes the fear of losing him was more intense than the fear and insecurity of him not loving me. A lot of time had passed by and I thought it was time for me to tell him how I felt. I had always heard that it is very hard for a girl to propose to a guy and generally it is the other way around but somehow I was not hesitant in taking a step forward. There were no inhibitions at all; in fact I was worried of his reaction towards me on saying such a thing to him. Confusion had set in by now. The boldest person I knew then was Ritika, and I knew if there is someone who could motivate me to express my feelings, it was her. We met and I told her about my feelings for him and the entire situation. She listened to the whole thing and then smiled silently, and there you go I blushed.

"You are so much in love with him" she said and smiled.

"Ok ok, enough. Now tell me what should I do now, should I tell him? Should I not tell him or should I wait for him to say something" I went on and on and asked her a million questions in one go with a big question mark on my face. Somewhere in my heart hopping that she will say yes.

'You idiot go and tell him, what have you been waiting for?"

And therefore I decided to tell him that I loved him.

We talked and talked, I could just not get over with talking about him. I just went on and on and on. It was time for us to go home now otherwise I would have continued talking about him, about us, our stories and how I loved him.

I reached home that night all lost in his thoughts and smiling away to glory. I now had to decide how to tell him, what to say, will he accept my feelings or will I land up ruining us forever. There were way too many questions in my mind and my thought process was now blocked and refused to work any further. I decided to keep it to myself for now and stay calm for the night and decide the next morning what I should do next. And what ideally should be my next step.

The next day I spent completely engrossed in thinking what I should do next and kept planning and thinking of different ways to tell him. One part of me insisted on me confessing my feelings for him, no matter what his reaction would be and without thinking will it be a yes or a no, I should not hide my feelings from him whereas the other part of me pulled me back from telling him anything, what if I lose him even as a friend. There were just too many thoughts and confusions.

I knew there was something between us, some connection, some feelings, just something. Otherwise a person like him would never open up with someone, share his problems or actually listen to someone and do as they say, but he did so with me. Who would stop a fight and back out in the middle if a friend asked him to? He did. Who would leave school friends because another friend doesn't feel they are the right people for him? He did. I had no reasons to think or convince myself with that he did not love me too, and I also knew that he being the person he is he will never come up and confess his feelings. He thought he was too cool to do that you see. And so I decided that I am going to tell him about my feelings and if he does not feel the same way I am not going to react greatly to it and will stay composed and carry on with our friendship without letting the relation we share get affected by the feelings which were new and god knows would persist for how long.

I called him up and we decided to meet up for coffee the next day. There were a lot of mixed feelings I was shuffling between, the feeling of loving someone, the fear of losing that person, the fear of what if he says, 'No I don't love you'. I barely slept that night. And then arrived the day that probably changed my entire life. For good or for worse I don't know.

I got up that day all set to tell my first love how I felt about him and that I loved him, to tell him that our friendship has taken another leap for me. I was all girly, cranky and weird that day. I just wanted everything to be perfect and things to get over with a blink of an eye. From clothes, to shoes, hair, kajal just everything. There was no scope of anything going wrong anywhere in my plan for the day.

I decided to wear my favourite denim skirt with black spaghetti and a yellow bag to go with it. Straight hair properly washed and set and every little detail intact. I was ready to leave. Mom had for sure smelled something fishy by then and she asked "What's the matter baby? All dressed up, nervous, extra particular about every little thing, where are you heading to?" you know they say when the daughter is in love the mother just knows.

"Nowhere mom, just going to meet up tuition friends" I said trying giving justification and trying my best to not make it sound like one.

"Oh so Akhil is also going to be there?"

"Yes ma, of course he will be there."

At that point of time I did not encourage any further conversation. One I was way too nervous to talk and two I knew I would spill the beans in a matter of seconds, and her reaction is what I have no idea off whatsoever. Even though I have the coolest parents in the world but still telling them that I am in love is like a big thing, I also wanted things to be clear between Akhil and me first and then of course telling mom and dad would have been the first thing I would have done, before that neither did it make sense to me to tell them nor did I have an idea of what should I tell them and how.

I left home and the entire time while walking to the cafe I kept thinking 'what should I say? How will I say it? How would he react to it?' It was the first time I had fallen in love and confessing it, was trust me harder than I could have imagined. Probably studying maths for the rest of my life would have been easier.

The logic behind the boy proposing and not the girl appeared to be making sense to me now. A bunch of red roses, chocolates, a cute soft toy and you are all set to propose a girl. But how do you go about the whole thing in the opposite scenario? I mean soft toys and boys are like a big no and I was confused. Stepping back and waiting for him to say something was not even an option anymore. So, then how ideally should I propose to him? I was having a hard time deciding what to do and so I called up Priya to my rescue and we went to archies. Very evidently the store was full of soft toys and cards, but dude I'm going to propose a boy. After a long search and a lot of options which appealed to me in the first instance but soon became a no, I found the ideal thing I would want to give him. A keychain, which could be split into two parts and each part could be kept by two different people. The one I chose was a heart. The heart would split into two halves. It has been the latest thing these days and so I decided to go with it. I hung one part of it on to my bag and put the other in a small packet to give it to him later.

My heartbeat was at a speed where I felt it would explode into pieces and my mind was getting numb. I definitely needed someone with me to support me and stand by me like my pillar, and once again Ritika was that person.

We were supposed to meet at Willows Bank for coffee. Ritika and I headed towards the venue and she kept pacifying me all this while. We reached there and found out that he was already there and to my surprise he was not there alone Anikait and another friend of his were there too.

"Thank god you came along Ritika, I would have died alone amongst these three men" I held her hand and said.

I was already so nervous and Anikait's presence only made it worse. Anyhow I composed myself and we went in and joined the gang. Everything was normal except for me. I introduced Ritika to the group and the other way around, after which we ordered coffee. We were talking in general about random stuff and people, and ritika being her, took care of the talking bit, which overshadowed my condition.

After sometime somehow Akhil and I started talking to each other through sms. Our conversation started with the partner's we had been looking for each other. I was trying to prepare him for what was coming his way. I told him I think I have found someone for him. We got so engrossed in our conversation that we did not realize we were sitting with other people around, and before we could think of being caught and avoiding such a situation there you go;

"Will the two of you please leave your phones for a while" said Anikait.

"Ya man, just texting a friend in Delhi" I justified.

"What about you goel?" asked Anikait in a very suspicious tone.

"A friend yar aur kaun" Akhil replied.

And just then Anikait threw a bomb on us;

"Will you both please stop texting each other" we looked at each other and it was written all over our faces that we were caught.

"No no, we are not talking to each other, are you mad or what" we both said in a manner which made it further more obvious that we were caught red handed.

"Show me your phone" said Anikait and snatched Akhil's phone. I skipped like 10 heartbeats in those two seconds.

"Smarty pants, you deleted everything na" wooh! A sigh of relief for me. Thankfully Akhil had cleared his inbox immediately after Anikait started the conversation, which now gave me enough time to do the same too. We then carried on with our normal conversation

Anikait being Anikait, god knows how noticed the key ring on my bag and says;

"Nice key ring Aditi" and with a smile I said thank you Anikait.

"But I have a question" he says and I knew exactly what he wanted to know.

"Where is the other half of the heart?"

It took me a moment to gather myself and answer to his query.

"It is with me only yar, I have kept it for the right person. I will give it to someone I love the most and would want to be with, all my life" and I looked at the key ring and then Akhil, he smiled and I was already smiling.

Hahahhaahha, laughed Anikait. From then on I silently sipped my coffee and so did Akhil. I guess he had got an idea of what was happening. Sometime later Ritika and I decided to leave, so we excused ourselves, said bye to everyone and left. All this while she kept pinching me "Tell him you idiot", but I simply walked out.

As soon as we left and came out in the open I called up Akhil and asked him to come out without telling anyone that he is coming out to see me. I was waiting for him, he sounded confused about the whole thing but he quietly came out. I asked Ritika to go ahead of me as I wanted to confess to him when it's just Akhil and me. I wanted it to be a moment when it would just be him and me; I did not want to say such a special thing in front of anyone. I did not want it to be taken as a light joke, because it was not one for me. I wanted the moment to be special and just between us.

I saw him coming out of the cafe. I stood there and watched him walk towards me, I fell in love with him all over again and this time, even more. By the time he was in front of me the entire world around me ceased to exist, all the chitter chatter of the people and the souls around just appeared invisible to me. For me all I could see or hear was him.

"Oye, what happened? He asked worriedly.

"Nothing as such, just wanted to talk to you about something"

"Ya tell me, are you ok?"

"Akhil, actually there is something I wanted to give you," he looked at me with a big question mark on his face "And promise me you will not laugh and will keep it with you all your life"

"Ok baba, I will not laugh and will always keep it with me, now at least tell me what is it?"

I took out the packet from my bag and gave it to him. He held it in his hand and looked at me. He could see the fear on my face and sense the love, nervousness and a mixture of those millions of feeling I was juggling with at that very moment. And from his expression and look, I could figure out that he too has got an idea of what is inside that packet.

He stuffed the packet inside his pocket and said I will go home and open it. It mattered a lot to me and I wanted to cherish his reaction on seeing the other part of the heart, forever. He agreed to open it and find out what was in it. My heartbeats were racing at a speed as if they were running in a marathon. I was nervous, scared and in a different world altogether. He opened the packet and poured out the thing in the packet on his hand. He looked at the other half of the keychain and then at my face, looked back at it again and then at me.

I looked at him, smiled, looked down and continued smiling and then closed my eyes looked up and said "I LOVE YOU AKHIL". I looked at him and it appeared as if he had just got the shock of his life, he froze for a while and stood there reaction-less. I then just turned around and started walking away.

All I could think off at that moment was that I loved him, for everything else I was numb. No fear, no questions, nothing at all. It was a beautiful feeling of love along with a relief of having told him that I love him. There was nothing I had to hide from him now. Nothing I had to pretend about, no hiding, hesitating or lying. Nothing was left unsaid. A big part of me was at peace.

CHAPTER 3

Walking away from there did leave a part of me at peace, but confessing my feelings also meant an answer to my confession. Of all I knew, I love you is either followed by an I love you too or no I don't love you.

I was not ready to listen to what it was, good, bad whatever; this feeling in between of nowhere was peaceful. For sometime at least I did not want to think of anything or any of the further consequences. I was in love and had confessed it, I just wanted to cherish that feeling and live with that high for some time.

Just walking away without asking or figuring out the next step was neither easy for me nor for him. I walked with a mixed feeling wondering about what would follow this confession and for him the entire thing came as a shock. He had never expected such a big leap in our friendship, and coming from me was a bigger shock.

Just 15 minutes later and I had not even walked a mile I called him up;

"Hi!!" I did not know what to say next, all I could do was smile, "Where are you?" I asked. I guess I was ready to meet him and listen to what he had to say. He was with his sister so we could not meet up, but we did happen to cross each other and there you go, that smile again. How beautiful can love be, no matter what situation you are in, how turbulent your emotions and you heart is, seeing that person could make you smile in any situation, and that is exactly what he did to me. He made me fall in love with him every time I saw him.

I was walking back home and I got a call from him;

"Hi" he said.

"Hey, what's up?"

"Nothing much, just got back home. You tell me what's up?"

"Nothing ya, just walking back home"

"Hmm"

"So did you like the keychain?', I asked him. He too knew that I wanted to know what he had to say, and he too wanted to answer it but someone had to initiate the entire conversation. I don't know why but I just asked him and did not even think twice before doing so. Did I do the right thing or not I don't know, I just asked.

"Yup I did" he replied.

"Akhil I know it came as sudden shock to you and is something neither of us expected, but what I said today is true"

"I know yar, why will you lie. But yar…"

"See goel, I love you, I can't force you to love me. All I know is that we are best friends and nothing can change that."

"Hmmm…. I hope so"

"I'm sure goel, it won't"

"But I don't feel that way for you Aditi,"

"I got that goel, and all I can do is accept it, respect your feelings and not let whatever happened today affect our friendship… right?"

"Yup right!, but I promise I'll always be your best friend."

Even though the last message I sent him that night where three similes, I was broken into pieces. He does not love me. I had lost my first love. I cried the whole night and slept it off. The feeling of the person you love not loving you back shook me. I had heard people saying that not being loved back by the person you love hurts. I could feel every bit of it now.

I was trying to come in terms with what had happened and things started to change. We did talk to each other but his messages became a rare thing and our conversations short. At the same time my expectations from him to understand that I'm trying my level best to keep our friendship intact only kept increasing, I had started losing my best friend too. It was killing me a little every day. Even then a part of me refused to get accustomed to it and I felt that it is just a phase and everything between the two of us will be fine, we just need to give it some time. In fact we just needed to give ourselves time.

One of these days we were having a word about his mom's health and he was pretty upset about it, she had been pretty unwell for a while now, I tried to calm him down and sooth him, I assured him to get him a good doctor's number as one of my mom's friend also had the same problem and that particular doctor had cured her and she was doing perfectly fine now.

The next morning I called him up, his phone was switched off and having kept trying for a long time I called him up on his landline. Uncle received the call and informed me that he is sleeping and that he would ask him to call me back as soon as he wakes up, on asking for Sunidhi too I found out that she was sleeping as well. I understood the fact and decided to call later.

By now I was getting accustomed to see our relation and the bond between us vanishing. Since childhood I loved sitting in small corners of the house. I was sitting in one such corner at home and fiddling around with the casio keys. Mom for a few days now had been asking what was wrong with me. She was sensing it somehow, but I always denied. Not anymore, I was in a different state altogether and there was no way I could fake it this time.

I could clearly see things falling apart and not just that, a sense of things just finishing between us was creeping in and only getting stronger by the day. At this moment I felt everything is just going to fall apart right away.

As I sat playing with casio keys, mom asked me a million times as to what was wrong and then I finally decided to call up goel that time and I did not talk to mom at that very moment as I knew if I talk to her I will say it all and break down. How hard we keep trying and keep giving things that are falling apart one chance after the other hoping that everything would just fall into place. And in this hope I kept trying to call him on his mobile.

This time he picked up the call and what came back as a reply was expected somewhere down the line. But it would be put across this way and in this tone was shocking;

"Hi, tell me? He said.

"Hey, what's up? Where are you?"

"I'm out with friends."

"Who?"

"Mahajan, but what's the problem?

"There is no problem baba, I called, because I just wanted to talk to you about something"

"What is it? What is wrong with you? What is it that can't wait? What is that you have been calling me since morning? Don't you get it; I don't want to talk you."

I was shocked, he had never spoken so rudely to me and those words were way too harsh.

"I have been calling you since morning to give you the details of the doctor for aunty's treatment, and moreover can't I even call you now or what?"

And it was only silence from the other end. That day and this conversation killed a part of me forever. A part which forever became silent. As I sat in the khopcha holding the phone in my hand, mom came in and saw me and asked me "What is wrong Aditi" and I started crying. It was as if I was just waiting for her to ask me and I could let all that pain out and cry my heart out. I did not tell her about me being in love with Akhil, considering the closeness mom and I share I'm sure she must have got it by now, I just told her about our friendship coming to an end.

If there was anyone I was close to as a friend it was him. Yes, he also eventually became a different part of my life too, but above all of that, he was my best friend and he was gone. For good or for bad I don't know but he was gone.

I tried calling him over and over again but he never replied. Sometimes from a different number, texting him with a different name but nothing worked, I spent nights in a row crying and waking up on a wet pillow.

It was time for me to leave Shimla and go to Mumbai. I had cleared the entrance exam for a Bachelors degree in Journalism and Mass Communication and after mom and dad having struggled a lot with their firm decision of sending me out, I was finally all set to leave, leave the place I had grown up and lived in for 18 years. The people without whom I would not even spend a day, I was heading for a new life altogether, the life I always wanted. To fulfil a dream I had worked so hard to achieve, and now when I finally had it I was not sure if I was ready for it. I was not sure if I can go out alone in the world considering the situation I was in currently. But somehow I left Shimla and reached Mumbai.

All our lives we keep dreaming about things we wish to have or achieve and how we would want our lives to shape up and one such thing is the university you would want to be in for your higher studies after 12th, everything was going as per the perfect plan I had in my mind. I had got into the college of my choice for the course I wanted to pursue since I was a kid. And there I stood in front of my dream. The university building and the name shining brightly 'Mumbai University'. The main building of the university. For a moment I completely forgot what all has been happening in the recent past, all I could see was my dream in front of me. A sense of pride and happiness had set in.

That moment did not last for long though. I was in a new place, where I knew nobody. It appeared to me like a new planet altogether. It was obvious that it would take me sometime to make new friends and adjust to the place, but the old friends who should have been at my back were also nowhere to be seen and then mom too left.

I was left alone to deal with all the circumstances that were to come. What I was scared of was not if or not I will be able to manage in the new place, will I get lost or what will happen to me. I was scared of being alone emotionally. Mom, dad and bhai were far away. All friends scattered and we could not keep in touch after class 10 only, and Akhil both my best friend and the man I loved did not want to talk to me. The thought of being so alone scared me even more.

The night mom left I sat by myself in my hostel room, cried a lot and then said to myself, 'I have worked very hard to get here, and now that I'm here I am not going to let this chance slip away. Even if all my friends are far and not in touch anymore and the only guy I ever loved does not even want to see me or care to talk to me I am not going to let it affect my purpose of being here. I cried a lot that day. I missed home and Akhil and wished he was there to tell me 'don't worry I'm with you, its time to live your dream Aditi'. I finally slept off with these thoughts and woke up next morning for the first class, my first day in college.

CHAPTER 4

Mumbai begins

I woke up in the morning all set to attend my first class at Mumbai Institute of Communication. As a student of Journalism and mass communication. My dream had finally come true and as I had told myself last night I have to live this to the fullest and not let whatever is happening otherwise let effect this part of my life which I had longed for and dreamt of all my life.

I entered the college and had a sense of fulfilment and contentment as I had landed where I had wanted to see myself and so did my parents, but somewhere down the line I was not happy, there was something which was pulling me behind and I was scared all the time, even when I was the happiest I was scared at the same time. There was something missing which was not letting me enjoy and cherish this moment of happiness. But I somehow managed to gather myself up and moved ahead. I tried making new friends and hanging out with people and it was happening as well. I had an amazing roommate, Crystal she was from Dubai and called me jam and also there were nice people living around and I was getting along well with them and things were going ok. Everything would be fine until either someone asked about me having a boyfriend and my best friend or I would see someone together, it always left me lost and shattered.

A month had passed by and I was managing pretty ok. I still tried to call Akhil every now and then and getting no answer to any of my calls or messages had now become a part of my life. With every passing day I was missing Akhil even more. Even if I would be with people around me Akhil would just be there in my thoughts and I would space out every now and then and if people would ask me what's wrong I would either land up crying or just say nothing and stand still and remain numb. I had started becoming very weird, not by choice tough, it was just happening. And as a result of which people had started pulling away.

I was unable to deal with any of this, I was away from home, Akhil refused to take my calls or message and I had no body that would understand me and help me through this. I had lost both my best friend and the person I loved at the same time. I could not even tell mom not that I was scared that she'll yell at me or something but I was scared that she would get too worried as she always said "God, never do this to my child that she falls in love with someone and he doesn't love her because she will not be able to take it" and that is exactly what had happened. I didn't want to worry her by the thought that I was not doing fine here by myself. So I decided to keep mum.

With every passing day I was only getting worse. I hardly ate and drank, whenever I sat down to eat Akhil would hit my head and I just could not eat anymore, I had started falling sick, migraine also started taking a toll. And then one fine day I landed up in the hospital unconscious. Well then they had to tell my parents. Thankfully Ajay was there that time. Ajay was a senior who was doing MBBS from there and was a family friend. He was a great help at that time and he informed my parents that I am extremely sick and have been admitted in the hospital. But I insisted that they should not come here and that I will manage and so they did not. I laid there unconscious for days together. All I would get up would be to go to the washroom and when the nurse injected me with something. Rest of the time I knew nothing that was happening around.

It was only after the 5th day I was able to sit up for a while and the first thing I wanted to know was did Akhil call. Of course deep down I knew the answer and when my friend told me, he hadn't I again started crying and so she called him and told him that I was really sick and am in the hospital from the past 5 days When my friend said he wanted to talk to me I was thrilled and suddenly a wave of energy hit me and I felt alive, but as soon as he kept the phone down it was the same again.

"Stop using these cheap stunts to get me back to you" these were his words with mahajan laughing in the background.

He thought I was pretending and lying so that he would think I'm actually sick and would talk to me, he did not believe me or my friends that I was actually sick. A day later I spoke to his mom and asked her to tell Akhil that all this was not a joke but is real and she agreed to do that.

Days passed by but he did not call. The doctors had finally discharged me and I was back in the hostel and had also started going to college. I was getting better. I was on medication but my food habits still remained the same. I could hardly eat or sleep.

CHAPTER 5

LIFE MOVED AHEAD

Even though I was back to college and following my daily routine somewhere it always kept disturbing me that how and why did Akhil never cared to call back or to find out how was I doing. One of those evenings I was just sitting in my room and my phone started buzzing and I thought as usual it would be mom to find weather I had dinner or not. But, the name I saw flashing on my phone that day was not mom it was Akhil.

I told myself, "Aditi stop dreaming and get real", but the very next moment I realised it was not a dream, it was Akhil calling after what felt like ages.

"Hello" I said and it sounded as if I was scared to even utter a single word

"Hi, Aditi, it's me Akhil"

And the ultimate silence creeped in.

"You there?" he asked to check if I was still listening or not.

"Ya ya," in a complete confused state ya ya is all I could say.

"How are you?"

"I'm fine, how are you?"

"I'm also fine."

"How are you doing now? How's health?"

"Hmmm.... it's better now."

"So how have you been all this while?" I asked

"Just been ok ya."

"Just ok?"

"Hmmm..."

"Yar Aditi I'm sorry."

"Sorry for what Goel?"

"You know it yar."

"Hmmmm."

"I should not have got influenced by mahajan and those guys, yes I freaked out for a while with the whole proposal thing, I could have taken time to get in terms with it but reacting the way I did especially the mahajan part was something I should not have done. I'm sorry yar."

"I'm glad you realised your mistake Akhil."

"Hmm."

"But I'm very hurt Akhil, I mean one, you just stopped talking without any reason, that too under the influence of that stupid mahajan, you know I'd kill him if I see him, bastard, and then when I was trying to get in touch with you, you just wouldn't."

"You remember I tried everything possible."

"I remember yar, I know I was wrong."

"Hmmm..." I did not know what to say or how to react. He had realized his mistake and was back, but what I had been through all this while was not something I could forget so easily.

"Goel tell me something, how could you even think I was lying about being in the hospital just so that I could talk to you?" and there was complete silence.

"You there?" I asked him to reconfirm.

"Han yar, I'm here. I just don't know what to say. Mahajan had just influenced my ability to reason to an extent that whatever he would say I would just agree to it. My own rationality and mind just didn't seem to exsist."

"Hmmm" I agree that your company can influence you and your actions but soo much that you start forming such views about your best friend. I was not sure about that. I was just not able to convince myself for this.

"Hello madam, what you thinking, enough now man, I said no I'm sorry."

"Hmm... alright, how have you been goel?"

It had been so long since we spoke to each other. He knew I was going to Mumbai but before he could get in anywhere we had fought, so I had no clue where he was and I really wanted to know where is he, what is he doing or what is he planning to do.

"I've been fine ya, I'm just sailing through."

"And college?" I asked.

"Yar that is what has made me go crazy. IIT or AIEE I couldn't get through any of them so now finally I'm going to chitkara, baddi."

"But you never wanted to go there" I said a little worriedly about what he must have been going through all this while. It's so strange how when you love someone the only thing that matters is if they are fine or not, no matter how much they have hurt you.

"I never wanted to, but no option." He said in a disheartened tone which made it clear that he was not happy with it

"Yea, all I can say is there is always a reason behind everything." I knew no words could pacify him or make him feel better so I tried to avoid talking about future and stuff.

We spoke for long that night, there was obviously so much to talk and catching up to do and during our conversation I found out the reason why he finally realised he was being influenced, Anikait had got into a good institute but he could not get in where he wanted to because he was foolish enough to get distracted. I guess it's only when you get a big blow you realise what you really have been up to all this while, until then no matter what anyone says or how much you keep hurting someone you just turn a blind eye to reality.

I was happy that he was back. My best friend was back. Things started getting back to normal. I was happier and started settling well now, he too was happy and glad that he realised his mistake in time. Even though he was back there was something missing somewhere. I didn't know what it was, but something was stopping me and holding me back from being what we used to be. I guess me and our relation just needed some time to get back to its original self. Our friendship and my love had just gone through a very tough phase we just had to give it time to heal.

It took a while for us to be our old selves. We started talking more often and gradually the authority we earlier had and the way we felt for each other was on its way back.

I'm glad we gave our relation time to heal because this time it's getting back stronger, may be because we knew how we were without each other and had realised the importance of each other in our lives and so we were extra careful and did not want to make any mistakes this time.

With time not only did we get back but our relationship also got stronger. It did take us time, but as it happened it was better and stronger than before. The calls and texts were getting back to how they where earlier. Things were smoother now. Not that I had forgotten or was suddenly out of love with him but having him back as a friend gave me so much happiness and satisfaction that for sometime I was fine with ignoring the fact that he was not in love with me. The reality that he was back but only as a friend was something I was aware of but did not want to think too much about it. I was happy with our relation the way it was.

The first semester was coming to an end and with it came along opportunities to go for internships abroad. I had always been very career oriented and wanted to grab any opportunity that came my way. We had a lot of interview's and I got through a couple of them but for some reason or the other things where not working out. By now Akhil too had settled down in college and had made good friends and was happy.

It was 7th November; I had an interview for an exchange program. I was nervous and a little worried about what would happen. I had been talking to him all evening to keep up my confidence and spirit. Right after my interview and getting a positive response and after calling mom and dad the first person I wanted to tell this was to him and so I gave him a call.

"Hi Goel."

"Hey wsup? How was your interview?"

"It was good." And before I could say anything he said;

"Hey, listen I want to talk to you about something."

"Ya say na, all ok?" I asked worriedly.

"Ya there is something I want to say, but I don't know how to say it" now this left me a little confused, what is it that he has to struggle so much to tell me.

"Tell me baba, relax don't worry" I assured him to make him comfortable.

"Ya Aditi I don't know if I should be saying this to you or not and this way, but aditi I am in love."

What?? I said loudly in my head, you're in love??? Like who? How? When? Where? Since when? I asked like a hundred questions in a second.

"Really?"

"Han yar, I don't know how and when but yes I am in love." I could make it out from his voice that he was smiling and happy about it. And in the silence that existed for a few seconds I skipped god knows how many heartbeats an thought to myself, Aditi I guess he too has fallen in love with you, is it you who he loves?

"Awww that's so sweet" I somehow managed to get back to the conversation.

"So why don't you go and tell her?"

"That's what I want to do but I don't know how. Will you help me?" Now this put me in doubt, why would he ask me for help to tell me he loves me. Does this mean...

"Ya ya sure, now tell me who is the lucky one?" I asked him.

"You know her ya, its Preeti."

And I froze. No, he doesn't love me, it's someone else.

"No tell me dude, should I tell her?

"Go you idiot just go and tell her and get her" I gathered myself and gave him a green signal. I had lost him all over again and this time not because he didn't love me but because he loves someone else. But one thing which gave me a lot of satisfaction and happiness was that he considers our friendship to be important and didn't let anything else affect that relation and told me about his feelings and the confusion just the way you would tell your best friend.

Our friendship and his relation both were just perfect. Time passed by and our friendship got stronger. He shared everything about his relation with me. Good, bad, problems and happy moments. He shared everything with me. Even if he had a fight with her he'd call me up and tell me and I would help him out to solve it. On one hand as friends it would be the ideal thing and on the other it was a little difficult for me to do this considering I was still not over him. Second year of graduation got over and we met. Our meetings always gave us memories to cherish. This time as I saw him from a distance and smiled, but he didn't react. I was confused and hit him as soon as I got close to him and said;

"Dude, where are you lost? You don't recognise me anymore or what?"

"Babe, Aditi, you look hot. You've completely changed."

That day for the entire time he kept looking at me on and off. It made me shy but I liked it and when our eyes met it was just magical. And the way he looked at me was so fulfilling. And such meetings helped us get through the next 6months.

CHAPTER 6

"When you try so hard but you don't succeed, when you get what you want but not what you need, when you feel so tired but you can't sleep" these words from a song by Coldplay is all that is crossing my mind. Its been almost three years now that I fell in the trap of love which today has become one such thing I just could not move apart from.

Final year of graduation arrived and things where more or less the same... the same Akhil and the same me. The only difference was how we grew even closer as friends despite episodes of rude arguments and fights. I guess this was something that kept me going. The comfort and calmness his emotional presence gave me had become my anchor which kept me hanging on and not sink.

Finally, the moment for which I had been putting in all the hard work and effort had arrived. It was time for placements or applications for further admissions for masters, in short the most awaited yet the most confusing moment in life. Just like most of the people my age I too was confused whether to take up a job or opt for higher studies. After a lot of confusion and apprehensions I came to the conclusion to pursue higher studies and not work for the time being and so I decided not to accept the job offers from aim high and cognizant and chose to go to Jaipur for MBA. Even though it appeared as if life was going smooth and on the right track without any tensions of an uncertain future there was hidden sadness and continuous feeling of confusion and unrest. The feeling of something missing and something going wrong, somewhere down the line kept poking me. I did know what it was but I tried to find million other reasons to try tell myself that the reason is something else. I'd pick up something or the other and get all cranky and vent out all my anger and anguish. And this only grew by the day. I could not hold it all inside me I wanted to let it out, scream, shout and go insane and just admit how hurt I was, but me being me could never do it. I'd cry by myself but could never admit it to anybody and tell someone how I was feeling exactly

The best way for me to run away from any kind of emotional stress or feeling is to involve myself into something so bad that I don't get time to even get tired, and that's exactly what I did. College clubs and their activities kept me so busy or rather I kept myself so occupied with them that I could not even find time to be upset or sad. Soon I realised I might be able to brush aside the thought of the pain inside me but could not get rid of it like this. It was within me and hurting me and affecting my life every single moment. Not paying any heed to it would just be like leaving a wound uncared for.

Akhil was still that part of my life which neither was I able to cut off and throw it nor was I able to keep it all to myself. It just kept going the way it had been going all this while. We would hardly talk but ya the time for us to meet up was always fixed. June and December. We always met during these breaks we both had in college. And where in Shimla

Mumbai came to an end. I left this place with a lot of experience and a bag full of knowledge which I would cherish for a lifetime. I felt myself to be at a completely different intellectual level, a place where I had always wanted myself to be in. what did not change was my emotional state, and it was still the same as it was 3 years back when I came to Mumbai. Or I could even say it was worse. I was unable to control or channelize my emotions anymore. The part of balancing yourself and not letting them affect the other aspects of your life had just gone completely missing. Emotions had overtaken me. Or rather I had lost myself to emotions, which without any doubt would be the worst place to land up in. The inability to take decisions for my own self was now becoming a characteristic of mine. The confident and independent me was lost somewhere. They say slow poisoning makes death even more painful, I'd say love made it even more painful for me. All these years love had been killing me slowly and without me realising earlier it had suppressed the real me and turned me into a vegetable cooked by love.

I don't know how I could make it sound a little funny but trust me, it was not at all funny. A senseless, clueless me had become the dominant part of my personality. The original I had just been swept away by the wave of love in a manner that I didn't even realise it until I found myself in an alienated state and did not know what was happening and didn't know the way out. I felt stranded.

I was now home after completing my bachelor's degree and to relax before I started with the next leg of my education that was MBA.

A major part of me did not want to go in for MBA and another major part did not want to work either, what in this case did I want? Well it was something even I did not know. After a lot of introspection I could tell this much that I don't want to do anything at all. I just want to be home, left alone and do nothing and just be. If only life would allow us to do that. I was very adamant that this is what I want to do and not an MBA or a 9-5 job. Two months of tussle between me and my new self but even then the solution I could come to was where I had started from, confused and uncertain.

My parents knew what I was capable of and that the right place for me was in a college pursuing MBA and not wasting away my life doing nothing and they made sure I did not do that.

I cribbed, cried, yelled, threw all possible tantrums but nothing worked and ultimately I was sent to Jaipur for my MBA. Even though I had been in the hostel for the past 3 years away from family and managing on my own it was of no help to me. I felt like I was this small kid whose parents were forcefully sending her to study in the hostel, and I cried like one too, refused to get off the car and the last one was not to leave dad's hand but all in vain.

He said "You have to make a future and you deserve this, what for do you want to sacrifice what you have achieved so far? People will stay and go but this is what will remain with you for life. Today it might seem very hard and next to impossible but when this phase passes away you will regret for having this opportunity pass away." He then hugged me and left and I stood there crying and thinking to myself that may be he was right. I was ready to put at stake the rest of life for what I had been going through. But did I have an option? Not really even if my mind would agree that I should concentrate on MBA I would just lose focus or interest in split of a second and go back to square one.

CHAPTER 7

Jaipur did not start on a positive note and my frame of mind had become such, that all I did was cry and keep insisting on going back. Making friends was the last thing I even wanted to think of. And the old ones, well I would just call them up and keep crying about me wanting to go back and eventually even they got tired of it. May be they were right on their part, but did they have an idea of what I was going through? The feeling of uselessness, worthlessness, failure, and recklessness had creeped deep within me and for someone to understand that, I guess I was expecting too much from them.

A few days passed by, I did make a few good friends which did not last long though. The irritable and unpredictable nature I had developed by now would just not be acceptable by anyone and once again I was left alone, abandoned by everyone at a time when I needed people around me the most.

Between all these things the only two good things where that I could now go home more often and also that Akhil was closer too and we were getting closer now and our friendship was only getting stronger. And I guess this was the time when my transition from unhappy to the happy me and adjusting in MBA happened. His presence was just so soothing and to know he's there would give me a reason to get up and start a new day.

It was October 18th, we were talking over the phone, I was to leave for shimla on 19th night for my birthday and wedding of a relative. I just said "Yar Akhil I wish you were with me this birthday." I really wished to celebrate my birthday with him but was always too far to make it practically possible. He was in Chandigarh these days and was in his final year of engineering, now that Jaipur and chandigarh were not too far I so hoped and prayed for my wish to come true. To the expression of my wish he replied and gave a completely unexpected answer. Something I could never assume he would say. "Well sure, I'll definitely try, if I get done early tomorrow I'll come to Jaipur and then we can travel back in your bus, I'll get off at Chandigarh and you go home." Just the thought of his doing so filled me with so much happiness that I was completely unable to gather my thoughts and react to it. He took down my bus booking details and after a while we hung up and slept off.

The next day he was caught up and not reachable till around 4:30, after which he called up and said that he had just got done and there was no way he could make it to Jaipur. There was nothing I could say to that and accepted it that he is not coming. I then got occupied with packing and getting done with all the formalities to leave the hostel and board the bus. It was on my way to the station that it came to my mind that may be he was just kidding and he has come over, but a second thought overtook this one too quick and I told myself "Aditi are you mad? Why would he do that? Has he ever in the past so many years made even the slightest of effort to do something for you and you think coming down to Jaipur would be something he would even give a thought to? This answered all my questions and I snapped out of my own sweet fairyland. Just like any other time I went home I boarded the bus and settled down. Somewhere a part of me was still hoping to see him there, and in no time the bust left. I tried brushing away the thought and sleep off. I kept thinking about how I was silly to even think of him coming. I tried to divert my thoughts by thinking about the wedding. I was excited, Punjabi weddings can be fun you know and when someone close to you is getting married it gets even better. With these thoughts after a while at around 10 I slept off and let sleep takeover my thoughts.

The bus reached karnal and stopped for dinner at Haveli. We pushed off from there at around 11:45 and as soon the clock struck 12, phone calls starting pouring in. Everybody called and so did Akhil. He did apologise for not being able to make it and wished me with great happiness in his voice and I too decided to understand that it was not in his control and he could no way miss an interview for his placement and come to Jaipur for a stupid wish of mine. We ended the call on a happy note and I too with a smile on my face like a chirpy birthday girl slept off.

I was so tired that I had no idea when it 3 was and we had reached our second halt, Barog. I was fast asleep and had no clue if the bus was moving or was at halt. It was only when suddenly the bus stopped with a jerk. I woke up and on looking out of the window I realised it was in the middle of nowhere and we had crossed Barog. In a matter of seconds the lights of the bus were switched on and I see someone walking in. I thought maybe someone wants to get off or is taking a lift, or sometimes even the drivers handed over parcels to people on the way but what I saw next was something I had not thought of even in the wildest of my dreams. I see Akhil walking on the isle with a cake in his hands and walking towards me. It took me a while to accept that he had actually followed the bus and traced it. He had been waiting at the regular halt of the bus where it did not stop that day and on finding that the bus had already crossed the place without a halt, he on his friend's bike drove all the way to hunt for it.

My eyes were still following the isle to convince myself that it is him when he politely asked the girl sitting next to me to shift to the seat behind us for a while and I screamed "Akhil? Is it you?" and before either of us could react he was sitting next to me. I was frozen, awestruck, beyond words and expressions and way too happy to even understand what just happened. It was followed by a hug and I asked him to pinch me, he laughed out loud and said are you ok? It was just too hard for me to believe that at 3:45 AM in the morning he had managed to track down the bus I was in and enter in with a cake. At 4 I cut my first birthday cake in the bus with everyone around watching with half opened sleepy eyes as to what was going on and on seeing the cake it was very well understood. It was the happiest moment of my entire life. Not because no one had done such a thing for me earlier or rather I did not let anyone come so close, but because it came from him. The feeling was just out of the world. And then from his bag came out a rose which again took me by shock. A red rose it was. And a statement with it;

"Dont get me wrong, I just couldn't find another colour." I took it and he hugged me and trust me when I say this, I was in tears, happy tears. After having loved someone for more than 4 years that person does something like this for you, all the pain I had gone through in the past years seemed too little. It felt as if everything I had been going through is now paying. All dreams would now come true. The love I had been waiting for is here. The rest of the journey passed away in this happy own world of mine. I just could not stop smiling and sleeping was way out of question. My happiness that morning knew no boundaries. On reaching home and seeing a cake and a rose in my hand mom and dad too understood where it came from and had broad smiles on their faces because they also knew what he meant to me and how much happiness this gesture of his would have given me. Another cake was waiting for me in my room and loads of gifts spread all over the bed. The entire day I felt like a princess. I felt the meaning of my name was best describing my life at this very moment in my life. Aditi- 'A bird with beautiful wings". And I too at this point had all the colours in life and was out there flying in heaven with the happiest heart. 20th October 2012. A date I can never forget in my life. A day when I felt my existence had a meaning. A day when for the first time the person I loved made me feel loved. The happiest day of my life.

CHAPTER 8

Everything now seemed very good and pleasant, life seemed to be getting better and smooth for a change. The convocation and final exams for the semester were over and we had a week's break before the next session started. And being in Jaipur had its own perks of being able to go home frequently. And home at this point in time had a different meaning all together, Akhil too would have been home and our bonding and relationship was at its best. I was too excited to meet him and spend some time with him.

His birthday had just passed by and I was out that day to get a gift for him. I was unable to decide what to pick up for him, so I decided to ask him if he had been looking forward to buy something and it would relieve a huge tension off my mind. But he did what he does the best which is just kept pulling my leg and beating around the bush. And then he said something which not only left me speechless but also gave a new hope for life "Mom is saying, no need of any of this, send the wedding outfit once and for all." He very confidently said to me. I was left speechless and went on to go buy his present which finally was a wallet.

I reached home and soon we decided to meet. The plan sounded amazing. Akhil was going to come home have lunch and then we would go out together. Well he being the shy person he is when it comes to family and relatives finally managed to escape the lunch and came home just for a while. The feeling of sitting with him at home among my family members was a beautiful thought in itself. After a while we left for a drive. We drove down up till kandaghat and back, the time we spent together during that drive was beautiful. And then he suddenly asks me;

"Oye, where is the ring you use to wear in your ring finger?"

I was not prepared for such a question. I had never thought he would even notice all these things.

"I don't wear it anymore yar, mom does not want me to give an image to people that I'm engaged or committed."

"But you're booked samjhi, for life." He said and I looked at him.

"No matter to who you get married and how many children you have we will still have an extra marital affair, because I can't live without you." And I just kept looking at him

"Why do we have to do things this way?" I asked.

"C'mon you known me ya, I am a twisted soul and he changed the topic."

All this made it so clear how important I was to him in his life and how even for him life will not be the same without me around. It just gave me a different kind of confidence of having him with me for life.

That one week just flew away and I had to go back to college but I knew I would be back again for Christmas and New Year. Those 15 days in college flew, and I didn't realize when it was time to go back home again. I reached home and the very second day I was asked by mom to clear out stuff with Akhil.

"Aditi we think you should now clarify things with Akhil. It's been so many years since you've been waiting; it's high time you get on one side of the road. For how long will you keep walking in the middle of the road?" Mom explained to me very carefully making sure I don't react to it very seriously.

I heard to whatever she was saying silently not sure whether I was ok with what they wanted me to do or not. It took some time to realize what I was being asked to do and what was coming my way. I knew this day would come I was sure about it, but what would follow that day post that conversation was something neither did I think of nor did I ever want to imagine. It was that part of reality which I ignored.

That entire day I sat down quietly in my room and everyone at home too gave me that space and time to think and decide how and when am I finally going to clear out things. After an entire day of complete silence from my end mom asked me "what's going on in your mind, unless you tell us what you are planning or thinking I will not be able to help you. What is it that is bothering you so much?"

"I don't know mumma… I don't know if I really want to talk to him about this. I don't know if I want this entire conversation to happen at all or not."

"But why bache?" Asked mom. "Don't you want to settle down with one feeling? For how long will you stay in this dilemma of having only a part of him? You know right things can't keep going on this way. You will have to decide right?"

"Mom it's just fine this way, I can't have this conversation with him. I just can't. Talking to him about this is like losing him."

"Why do you think you'll lose him, instead we think even he loves you."

"But mom what if he again says no?"

"Bache but at least you will know the final call, because if he still hasn't fallen in love with you or is not ready to accept his feelings he never will. It's been 5 years."

I had now finally decided that I will clear things out with him and there is no more putting things off, especially this.

CHAPTER 9

The final confrontation

It was 25th December, Christmas and we had gone to one of mom's friend's house for a day out. We had a nice day. Goel and me had been having a chat and were deciding to meet up in the evening. We all from auntie's house went to the mall. Aunty and her children wanted to visit the church and we too wanted to take a walk. We reached there and after a while Akhil and me met up. Mom decided to head back home and I decided to come back with dad. Well we now had enough time in hand to talk and enjoy. We were still roaming around when I started the conversation

"Yar goel I wanted to talk to you about something."

"Shoot ya" he said.

"Not here and this way, it's something serious."

"Hahaha.. Dude are you serious? You're getting married or what?

And I kept quiet.

He looked at me and said "Whaaattt? You're getting married…?"

"Akhil" I looked at him and he shut up realising I'm serious.

"Nooo, im not getting married just yet but you know everyone at home asks, and I keep saying no and you know the reason why." There was complete silence and we kept walking. We reached near clarkes, and stood there.

"I don't know what to say yar" he said.

"What ya akhil, who other than you would know?."

"Aditi can't we have a way out? I can't lose you, but you also know right I am not even settled yet."

"Who is asking you to get married goel, all I'm asking you is an answer, a commitment."

"But how can I say anything at this moment."

"Ok let's do one thing lets meet up and sought this out, because this time we will have to. There can't be any putting it off this time."

"Hmmm." After we walked a few steps he asked me;

"Do we have to have this conversation?"

"Yes goel we have to, it's high time, and this time even mom dad are adamant about us clearing out stuff."

"Hmmm"

"Cool then we meet up for lunch tomorrow and talk things out."

"Hmmm ok. I'll let u know." he said.

"Goel it could be the last time we meet up tomorrow," I said this and had tears in my eyes.

We hugged to say bye and when I looked at him and he looked back at me in my eyes he too had tears, and a mixture of love, loss, fear and a whole lot of emotions. I could tell he too was equally worried and disturbed.

I just turned away and walked back home but this time not looking back.

That day when we said bye and good night it was a different feeling and heart ache altogether. A pinch in the heart on saying bye to something very close to my heart. But I chose to ignore that feeling and told myself 'Aditi don't start assuming things. You are going to meet up tomorrow and talk it out. Don't think too much. Well if only not thinking about it was possible, in fact all I could do was think about him and where our relation which was a mess already heading too.

I met up with Drishti and had a drink, there was no other way I could have calmed down a little. And after that I went back home and without talking much to anyone I just got into my bed and cried. I told mom that I had a drink and want to be left alone by myself. She did that and I cried in my bed. After everyone had dinner mom came to my room and asked me

"What's wrong bache? You both where together right, what happened? All ok?"

"Yes mom we were together, I have initiated the conversation, we are going to meet up tomorrow and clear things out."

"You want me to sleep with you today?"

I refused but she knew I needed her by my side so she decided to sleep with me that day.

"Talk to me bache, that is the only way you will feel better."

"What to say mom, we are meeting up for lunch tomorrow and clearing things out."

"Then what is troubling you?"

"Mom it's all coming to an end, having this conversation with him, clearly means putting an end to us. Our friendship, relation, love, and the hope of him coming back someday. I know if we have this conversation tomorrow we are over."

"But you can't be living in the situation you are right now."

"I don't know mumma, but letting him go is not something I can do easily. I love him mumma. He's the only guy I've ever loved, I have never let anyone come close to me or enter my life. All I've done is waited for him to one day finally realise that he loves me. Because I know he does love me. Everyone around him and me also know that he loves me; he just does not realize it. It is just that one fine day for him to realize. I want to wait for that day mom."

"Even we think that he loves you beta, the day he had come home both your brother and me felt that he too has feelings for you"

"Really?"

"Yes, the way he looked at you and talked to us even when he was looking at you, it was very evident. That is why we have been forcing you to have a conversation with him and clear things out."

But maa he doesn't agree to his feelings. He has still not acknowledged his feeling. He still thinks he doesn't love me. He says I am just a very good and a special friend. He stills sticks by the fact that we are best friends and that's it. If we have this conversation tomorrow it is going to be the end of everything.

The end of love,
The end of me having waited for him for all these years.
The end of having loved him selflessly,
Having done everything possible to make him happy.
And the end of me, mom.

I am not ready for this maa, I don't know if I can survive bidding him a final good bye."

"We are with you bache, to hold you and support you, but you have put this on one side of the road.

"Hmmm." Is all I could say and I started crying, and tried sleeping. That night I hardly slept all I did was toss and turn or else wake up scared suddenly. Nothing had happened yet and this was my condition, god knows what would happen when we actually met.

The next day Goel did not take my calls until evening and I knew this is it, we are never going be talking again, but I kept trying and finally he answered the call at around 4 in the evening and apologized and said he was out with family and friends. And as a co incidence that very day I met him on the mall in the evening. He was with tarun. We met and tarun says;

"I'm sorry yar I ruined your date."

I looked at him and then at goel." C'mon man what date? Couples go for dates, not friends "And he looked kind of shocked.

I told goel that listen we are definitely meeting up tomorrow. We can't avoid it. "Ya we'll see." He said and we left.

Next day in the morning I called him and asked him "So see you at willows for lunch?"

"No ya, lunch will not be possible but will see you at around 2."

"Ok cool."

Somewhere I still had the hope that we will not have this conversation and everything will just be normal like it was a few days back. And sitting in my bed I just didn't realize when it was already 1:30. I called him up to find out where were we going to meet up.

"I'm a little stuck at the moment aditi, I'll meet you later."

"Goel I don't know we have to meet up today, you can't keep running and avoiding this I'm not listening to anything. Where are you?"

"I'm at willows playing pool with friends."

"Ok cool, you play abhi I'll see you at 4 at willows."

"Cool done."

I kept the phone and realized it was here. Things were now coming to an end. The day I had been dreading for the past so many years is here and that there is not going to be any avoiding or putting it off this time. Another 2 hours to go and we will be face to face having a conversation, in short putting an end to us.

I could hardly breathe, and was completely numb. I got ready, zipped up my jacket and was about to leave, when mom came in and gave me some money, my phone etc and said "I have called up drishti, she is coming to take you and will be there with you all the time."

"No mumma I want to talk to him alone."

"Ok bache she'll wait outside but she will be with you."

"Hmmmm."

Just when I was about to leave mom says ;

"Be confident and clear everything out this time beta, we all are with you. If he loves you get him forever and if he still does not have the courage to accept his feelings free yourself from having waiting for him. It is going to be tough, but we are with you. We will do this together and deal with it."

I couldn't say anything and I left.

I have no clue about how I walked up the hill to meet Drishti and then head to willows. I was only getting more and more numb, my hands cold and still sweating, my face completely pale and numb and completely lost and clueless. As soon as I met Drishti she shook me and said "Aditi are you ok?"

"Yup, shall we go?" I said and walked towards willows.

All along the way she kept giving me instructions

"I'm going to be right there outside, any point in time you feel you need me just give a call and I will come in. Don't stay quiet this time, say all you want to, and be bold." And she went on and on and I don't remember most of what she said. I was completely zoned out.

We reached willows; it appeared as if Drishti just carried me there. I called him and told him I'm here and he came up. The moment I saw him I skipped a beat. It was a very mixed and weird feeling. The feeling of meeting the guy you love and at the same time having a strong feeling that this could be the last time I'm meeting him.

Drishti left me and Goel and I went inside the coffee shop. We sat down in our favourite corner and just looked at each other.

I somehow gathered courage and said "lets order something, they will kick us out otherwise"

"Hahahah, he laughed and said.

"You order I don't want anything."

"I don't want anything either Akhil."

I ordered coffee for both of us.

"Order only one" he said and I did so.

"So Say?"

"What do I say?"

I was not able to breathe, I was cold and numb.

"Aditi say something."

"Say what goel? Not like you don't know the reason we are here for and the conversation we are suppose to be having."

"I know yar but at least say something."

"I love you" are the first words that came out of my mouth and that's all I could say.

"I know that, hmm."

"I know that you know I love you goel, but the point is I've been waiting for all this while and you know it. I want an answer Akhil."

"Answer for what aditi, I've said it, we can't be together."

"But then what was the relation we shared all these years? Please don't say just friendship. Everyone around us except for you thought we are a couple, including your friends and our families. You yourself have told your friends when you have been drunk how you felt about me. Why is that you could talk about only me when you were drunk and not anyone else? Why is it so, that you would listen to anything I say and never say no. Why am I so important for you? Why is it that you can't be without me? Why is it that even after we get married we are still going to go on dates? Why is that even when you weere dating someone else you would share your feelings only with me? Why is it, that your sister addresses me as bhabhi to her friends? Why did you come back when I had asked you to leave? Why would you travel at 3 at night in the cold with a cake in your hand? Why am I the one who understands you more than you understand or know your own self? Why goel? Why? Have you asked yourself this?"

"Aditi I've always told you all this was just as friends."

"Akhil I used to think it is me who needs to stop waiting, but everyone can't be wrong right? Everyone around us feels you love me. Everything you do shows clearly you love me, but why is it only you who does not agree to it?"

"I don't know yar."

"You have to akhil. It's been 5 years. It's a long time goel. Really long. And every time we pull apart you give me hope of being together."

"Aditi I guess we need to part ways. This is the last time we are meeting up and it's all over. We are not going to keep in touch anymore."

"But goel?"

"Yes Aditi. I'm going to leave as soon you finish this coffee. That is it. Its over Aditi." All I could do was cry and cry.

I sat there and kept crying.

I begged and pleaded. Said everything I could.

"I can't live without you goel and you know that."

"You can Aditi."

"I can't goel, I might just breathe but I will not be able to live, don't do this goel please don't do this."

By now I was broken and shattered. He was about to leave when I asked him "Can we have a picture?"

"No" he said. "You are going to keep it with you and cry every time you look at it and will never move on."

"Goel when you know every time I see it I will cry and never move on so then why are you doing this? You know I will not be able to live without you, you know that I love you and you know I will never be able to love anyone else ever, then why do you want to leave goel."

He stood up and was leaving when I asked" Can I have a hug?"

"Yup, that you can" and I hugged him, I hugged him so tight as if on doing that I will be able to hold him back and he will not go. And I cried and cried and cried. "Please don't go" is all I could say.

"I have to go Aditi its time."

"No goel, I will not be able to live."

Tarun walked in then and also asked goel to think over it but he refused

I kept hugging him and gripped him even tighter. "Goel pleasee don't go…."

He started pushing me away, I was holding him soo tight that it was difficult for him to do that but he finally pushed me away and he left.

I screamed "Goel please stop…"

And he left. I fell and tarun held me and calmed me down a little. I ran after him and yelled out his name and hugged him. By then drishti too came and saw me crying and hugging him.

Akhil pushed me away and Drishti pulled me back and he left. Somehow Drishti managed to make me stop crying and called up dad to take me home. Dad held my hand and walked me back home. I walked back home and even today

I don't remember taking that walk back home I was so numb and still, dad somehow managed to drag me home.

As soon as I reached home mom saw my face and figured out what had happened. I straight away went to my room and sat down on my bed. Mom gave water to dad and came to my room. I was sitting there with lights off just like a statue and crying.

"What happened baby?" She asked me.

I did not say anything and she shook me and asked loudly what happened Aditi, dad heard mom shouting and came to my room and as soon as I saw dad I hugged him and burst out in tears.

"He left dad. He's gone. Everything is over dad, everything is over. I loved him. He does not. He's gone dad. I love him. Please get him back dad I can't live without him papa, I want him back." I just hugged dad real bad and howled more and more and sat down. Mom held me and I cried even more and more. "Mumma please get him back. Please papa. I love him papa, I love him a lot, please get him back, he's gone dad. Please do somethng. I want him back dad."

I cried and cried. And mom said, "He's gone Aditi and he is not coming back."

"I don't know mom, I want him back. You know maa how much I love him. I've always loved him mumma. He also loves me but does not accept it. Do something na so that he realize he too loves me."

Bhai too came to the room and I hugged him and cried even louder. "Bhai he left, please do something."

I kept saying these words. But all in vain. Nothing was going to happen, he was gone and this time it was forever. I cried that entire night.

The next morning I woke up with swollen eyes, quiet and numb. It was like the silence after a huge storm. For me it was a storm. Akhil was gone. It was the last time I met him yesterday. There was not going to be anymore seeing each other.

Akhil was gone.

The only guy I ever loved and can ever love was gone. I sat in my bed lost and clueless. I had no idea where I was. Everything seemed so weird, nothing seemed correct, I was senseless and not thinking logically or for that matter just thinking was just not possible for me.

When you love someone, keep loving them even when they don't, they hurt you and you still keep loving them, they love you and you love them even deeper, they give you hope of being together some day and you keep loving and waiting and then one fine day they leave you and kill you and you still keep loving them.

The day when it was raining and we stood outside cafe soul and I buttoned his cuffs as he was hurt and we had to prevent the bandage from getting wet, the way I looked at him and he looked at me kept flashing in front of me. I would smile remembering that, how we would hug each other when we met, those days on the mall, the long drive, the birthday cake, the way he looked at me, the way I would skip a beat on seeing him or talking to him, the day I realized I love him, I smiled as everything flashed back and that very moment reality struck me, that love, that friend, that time, that relation, that wait is all gone and what is left is a broken you and memories. Everything else is just pain and more pain.

I met him as a friend, fell in love with him, but he didn't love me. We still remained friends and I still loved him. Sometimes he wanted to part ways and sometimes I wanted to, but we never did. Sometimes he knew being in touch is not good for me and sometimes I knew, but one thing neither of us could ever answer was. "When you lose a friend, the person who you love supports you, and when you lose the one you love your friend supports you, but what do you do when both these people are the same? What do you do if you lose both the person you love and your best friend at the same time? Who do you look up too?

And at this point of time I had lost both and did not know what to do. I was lost and felt stranded. In a situation when the most experienced would not know what to do and would be left clue less.

The next day was only getting worse. There are times when you sleep with the hope that when you'll wake up next morning you'll realize it was all just a dream and is over, but sadly it was not a dream but reality which stood in front of my eyes and I wished I could just shut them and go back to sleep again where I could at least tell myself that all this may be is just a dream.

Everyone at home was trying their best to make me happy and distract my mind. It was not even funny how bhai came to my bed with my hair straighter and asked me to straighten his hair. I was taken aback with the care. Bhai would never let anyone even touch his hair. Straightening them was out of question, he even did that to change my mood and bring me out of last night's incident.

I was still in that very moment and still struggling to register what had happened. The mathematic calculations in my mind just refused to give an answer and stated an error, but deep down I knew what had happened and what was on its way.

Everything is now a little less,

I smile less,

I laugh less.

I eat less,

I work less.

I dream less,

I chase dreams less.

I aim less,

I want less.

I think less,

I grow less.

I live less,

I care less.

I love less,

I let someone love me a lot less.

He's gone and this time forever. I don't want him back ever now for what he has left behind is, "A lot less like me, a lot less of me."

CHAPTER 10

They say pain eases out with time, I didn't know about the time aspect but yes when with family things definitely become a lot easier. Somehow I gathered myself and was trying to be as normal as possible. It was 31st December and we were going to bring in the New Year at The Destination. One of our favourite places. I tried occupying myself with the weirdest things possible. That day at the party I just wanted to go numb to be able to be at ease at least for some time. For a while I wanted to just relax and have no thoughts crossing my mind, which was very difficult but after two three drinks it just gets fine. That night I was fine and the next day I had to leave for Jaipur as college reopened on the 2nd.

This time I choose day travel. One because at no cost did I want to see that bus where I had the best moment of my life and two because the fog had resulted in delaying of the busses. It was not at all the right choice to make, but then when did I ever make the right choices. Everything I had done this far just seemed completely useless and I felt so worthless. Even though there was no fog during the day the bus took way too long to reach. By the time I reached my pg I was dead tired. I just washed my face and hit the bed. I just wanted to sleep and had no energy to stay up anymore.

As soon as I closed my eyes I was surprised how I was not sleepy anymore. No I didn't want to get up and eat or do anything else but I also could just not sleep. I just lay down still, with millions of thoughts crossing my mind. Of Akhil, about our friendship, about how everything just got over and the possibility of things still working out. I didn't sleep the entire night which made it impossible for me to make it to college the next day. Thankfully that day it was only registration and they would have carried on for the entire day and so I decided to go in the afternoon and finally slept at around 5. I reached college at around 1 and got done with the formalities, found out the schedule for the classes which started the next day and then came back home and again lay down in my bed.

I just didn't feel up to anything. Just nothing at all. I just wanted to lie down and be there. No music, movies nothing at all. Everything just irritated me and annoyed me. Silence was the only thing I liked. I guess because there was so much chaos inside me that any activity outside would just cross the threshold of my tolerance power. I lay in my bed for the entire day untill Ritika who stayed in the other room came back from work and knocked at my door. It was then that I finally got out of my bed, ate something and unpacked my stuff. That night again I didn't feel like eating anything. I just had curd and slept off.

Next morning again I had to force myself to get out of bed and go to college. I met roshni ma'am and got some energy. She was the only reason I went to college. Had she not been there I wouldn't have even come back to Jaipur. Her presence gave me so much support. She did not have any clue of what was going on. But still, the encouragement I got from her to stand up confidently was motivating enough for me to get up and go to college every day. For the next one week or so I was happy and energetic enough for going to college. I could just manage pulling myself out of bed and attend my classes.

I would quietly go to class, sit through the lectures and come back home. Not talking to anyone, no noise nothing just silence. Sit through the lectures for 4-5 hours without even talking to anyone, just by myself or at the most listen to songs and sit alone during breaks. I could by the weird looks of my classmates guess how they thought I was weird or probably going crazy by the day. Of course it mattered what they thought of me but after a few days even that didn't affect me anymore. The feeling of I don't care had become my thing by now.

At this point the only person I would talk to was Abhi. He was my junior in college and both of us where a part of the literature club and had the old Mumbai connection. And somehow during this phase we got even closer. It was only if I met him I would feel like being right there in the moment. But that too lasted only a few days.

The original me was lost. Someone who would have so many points to raise in class just sat down quietly. But what happened one day in class forced me to think of what was going on. No, this was not the first time it was happening. Earlier too the teacher asked me questions and I just didn't have an answer, and even if I knew the answers I just could not put those thoughts together or frame them into sentences and give the answer and if at all I would be able to frame them and put all the strength in standing up and answering the moment I would start speaking "Blank". No words would come out of my mouth and would stand mum.

The best class was that of my favourite subject behavioural science. I was fond of both the subject and the teacher and would be full of energy in her classes but when the same happened in her class I was forced to do something about it. For an entire week I kept on thinking of what to do and finally after a week I went and spoke to the same teacher, Priya ma'am and told her that I need help and that I'm not doing fine. She then guided me to meet Charu ma'am. A counsellor. I told about this conversation with ma'am to Abhi and he too said "Adi, we must go and see her na then, when we a have a solution and help for a problem why not."

I was confused about it and was not able to decide what to do and so I kept putting off the thought and the decision.

It was one of those regular days when I had come back from college and was damn tired and the day had been a little difficult one. So, I just wanted to lie down in my bed and just be. The day past by and it was around 5 in the evening and I didn't even realise. I was very restless that day. I don't know why but nothing seemed to calm me down today. I just kept tossing and turning or going up and down in my room. Every moment of 27th December kept crossing my mind, those words, that feeling everything. I somehow could not get control of the feelings and the thoughts crossing my mind. I was trying, trying very hard to control myself or let those emotions out. I wanted to cry but just couldn't, wanted to scream but no voice, wanted to talk to someone but didn't know what to say and how to start. I felt stuffed as if someone had just tied a piece of cloth around my face and left me with no air to breathe. A moment finally came when I opened my mouth to try grasping some air to breathe. The strangled feeling was too much to take and neither did I know how to deal with it nor did I have an idea about what should I do to get rid of this state. Suddenly I got up from my bed, reached out to my study table grabbed a cutter I had been using lately for the college fest and slid it through my wrist leaving a deep cut and I didn't realize how long I kept doing that unless I saw blood all around me and my phone started buzzing. Abhi was calling to find out how was I, it was with the ring of the phone that I was able to come back to my senses realizing what had I done and that is when I started feeling the pain and could finally breathe.

"Hi adi, how are you?"

"I'm fine Abhi."

"You don't sound fine though, what's wrong Adi?" He asked, somehow sensing something was not right.

"Abhi I just realized I harmed myself" and again I entered this numb state. He kept instructing me and I like a robot did as he said and cleaned the wound and slept off.

The next morning I woke up and left for college trying my best to cover the wound which was now paining and bleeding at intervals, after the first class I met abhi, he had got the medicines that would be needed to do the dressing. As he dressed the wound I just looked out of the window and didn't want to look at the wound. It was hurting but at least I could feel the pain, it felt better, the weird pain which I could neither feel nor get rid of was gone. A sense of actual pain somehow didn't leave me struggling to breathe.

That day finally he forced me to ask Priya ma'am for the number of the counsellor and meet her, because things had now got out of hand and I was not going on the right track. It was only getting ugly with every passing day and there was no more delaying that could be afforded.

At around 4 pm I was standing outside Charu madam's cabin waiting for her to call me. Abhi was with me and kept consoling me and telling me that we are doing the right thing and there was no harm in talking to her and getting treated. I was somehow still a little hesitant but he was sure that today there was no going back from here and we were going to talk to her today.

As we entered her cabin I saw a smiling face with a bindi and tied back hair and an aura which was welcoming and more importantly comforting. I just quietly went in and sat down... I didn't want to say anything or rather I didn't know what to say at all. So I decided to just go in, sit and wait for either Abhi or ma'am to initiate the conversation.

"Yes bache, what happened my dear?" she asked me with a smile and politely expecting me to speak. I just looked at abhi and then her and then looked away. What should I say? Am I good? No. Am I doing just fine? I don't know... Am I in a bad shape? I guess. In a situation where I myself am not sure how I am how could I explain it someone else.

Just when I was struggling to gather my thoughts and say something Abhi spoke up.

"Actually ma'am there is a problem which brings us here, we knew she had not been doing well from some time, we have been trying to handle it ourselves and we were able to manage up till now, but now things have gone beyond our control."

"But what is wrong my dear?" Ma'am asked worriedly wanting to know what really was wrong?

"Ma'am she has been in depression but recently she has been showing symptoms of bipolar disorder, but what brings us here at such a short notice is that she harmed herself yesterday. That freaked me out and I decided that without any further delay we will be visiting you today itself, as today it was cutting her wrist but it could have been worse and we can't be taking any risks with her life."

"You did the right thing Abhi, I'm glad you're here. But now I have to speak with her alone and hear her out." She politely asked Abhi to step out and he left. There was pin drop silence in the room. I just kept staring at the floor quietly. Ma'am didn't interrupt my thoughts for like 5 minutes and then finally asked;

"What are you thinking bache? What's going on in your mind?"

"I don't know, just too many things."

"Ok, don't worry, just tell me the thing that is crossing your mind at this very moment."

"Why did I harm myself? What has happened to me? What have I become? Why do I still love him?" and I was out of breath.

"Calm down Aditi, let's take this one at a time starting from the last thought. Do you still love him?

"Yes, I do and there is this constant wait and hope that he will realise one day, someday."

"You are not in talking terms with him?"

"No, we haven't spoken in almost two months."

"Why? What happened?"

"We decided to part ways because he refused to accept his feelings for me and I had been waiting for him for 5 years and so we haven't spoken since 27th December."

"That's a very bold decision you made, and you know right that it was very much required for you to take this stand. It will definitely take time for you to come in terms with it, but you did the right thing my dear."

"I don't know ma'am, he was the only one I ever loved, I didn't let anyone come into life and kept waiting, he gave me all the hopes of loving me someday and now suddenly it's all over. Somehow I still feel it's one of those fights which will get over and he will be back. But I've lost him. My first love, my best friend."

"How did you lose your best friend?" She asked with a confused look.

"He was my best friend and now that he's gone both of them are gone" and I burst into tears or should I say I started to howl. She didn't stop me from crying and I kept speaking my heart out and crying and crying. It was after 45 minutes or so that I calmed down slightly after telling her what had happened last night.

"Can I see the wound? If you are comfortable?" she asked.

I just quietly pulled my sleeve up and put my arm across the table and looked away.

"Did you see the doctor kid? They are pretty deep and should be bandaged properly" She inquired with a scared and worried look on her face.

"No I didn't see the doctor, they would ask too many questions and I don't even want to go and see them, so Abhi had put some medicines"

"Ok, but promise me that you will bandage it properly or else the wound will go worse."

"Hmmm."

"Ok, tell me one thing, have you told your parents about this?" She asked.

"They know everything about Akhil, they do know I am having a tough time to get over him and am low but they don't know the extremity of the situation." I said.

"Don't you think you should tell them, before it gets too late?"

"But how do I tell them? They will be shattered, I can't do this."

"But don't you think they will be more hurt if in future something worse happens?"

I did know she was right but telling mom, I mean how to do that and what to say.

"What is stopping you? Are you worried they will not understand?"

"Noooo, I know they will, it will be difficult for dad to accept it but mom will handle him"

"Then what is stopping you?"

"I just don't know how to say it to her. It is very hard for parents of a kid like me who has always been so confident and outstanding to find out this about their child."

"You have to beta, now today you will go home and tell mom, okay?"

"Hmmm, ok." I agreed to what she was saying.

"But how will she react? What if the reaction is something completely unexpected? I mean out of proportion kinds, what if she panics?"

"You said that your parents are very understanding and open"

"Yes they are."

"Then why are you so worried, they will surely understand then. It's nothing but the fear in your mind that is stopping you from taking this step."

"I don't know if it's the fear or the guilt of having taken this step which is holding me back, but I guess a smart move would be to tell mom everything and not delay it any further, so I will call her today and tell her everything and I'm sure she will understand and not overreact or act out of proportion."

"Now that's like my girl, very good."

At last I took a deep breath, felt slightly light and this comfortable feeling was there of someone rational, elder, experienced and the right person being there to guide me and support me. I left her cabin in a better position than that I came in with. I had decided that I will go back to the pg today and tell mom.

C'mon Aditi, she's your mother, like your mom, your best friend mom, the super cool one why are you so worried? Hasn't she understood you so well this far. Even though I had a lot of contradicting thoughts in my mind as this is something any parent would freak out after listening to but I kept telling myself that no, mom will understand and the fear is just in my head.

I went home that day and after changing and stuff I called up mom and told her each and everything, like everything. From how I had been feeling, the struggle in the classroom, the low confidence to harming myself last night and my visit to Charu ma'am. I just let my heart out to her and told her each and everything.

"Hmmm... somewhere I knew that you were going into depression, we knew you were having a hard time coping up with what ever happened but I didn't know it had reached the extent that you would harm yourself."

And I started crying.

"Don't cry baby I can understand that it's not your fault, don't worry now that we know there is a problem we will take care of it and handle it and you will be fine."

I felt relieved. Just having told her gave me a feeling of being so safe and the problem being half solved. What followed next was quite expected, counselling sessions, breakdowns, and high moments. Just like it is for a bipolar patient one moment you're extremely happy and the other moment terribly sad.

They say right whenever you are in trouble god sends in someone to be there with you. My angel had been around me all this while but somehow we never got together. I don't know how and why one day I shared everything with her and she just hugged me and said "I love you darling." Roshni Ma'am, my guardian angel. It had been almost a year since she was around I did have a good clicking with her, but when the harming incident happened I don't know why but I just felt I had to tell her and somehow had the feeling that she would understand. The way she looked at me always gave me a feeling that she knew that there was storm inside of me and was just waiting for me to open up to her myself and just when I did that I just had to say a few lines and the rest she just knew it. She is elder to me I mean a lot elder to me, but the comfort zone I was in when I was with her was something different altogether. She was more than a teacher, not just because she was with me in my difficult time but because I admired her for being what she is. Bold, though, soft and there to support anyone who needed her no matter how that person would treat her she would just be there to support anyone in trouble.

Initially, I felt just like she would do it for anyone else she is supporting and helping me too, but in sometime I realised no. It was the love and bond that we formed because of various reasons and the fact that she could see and feel what I was going through that had got her close to me.

Not only did she support me emotionally but also helped me get homeopathic medicines to deal with the situation. She would call up day in day out to find out if I was having them on time. She knew I was staying alone and eating food was the last thing I would do and the state I was in would have further led me to not eating anything. She made it a point that she got me something or the other to eat in the morning and either made me eat it in front of her in her cabin or got something I could eat on my way to class. She just made sure I ate. And now and then between the periods she would just pass by making sure I see her because she knew seeing her would calm me down and also she would be worried if I was doing fine or not.

I had gone home for the weekend. I had thought mom will talk to me about my state or at least ask me about my wounds and will ask me to show it. But nothing of this sought happened. They behaved completely normal as if nothing at all had happened. Neither did mom ask how I was doing nor was she interested in knowing how were my wounds. I mean I understand they didn't want me to feel awkward or guilty so she did not want to see them but completely ignoring the fact wouldn't have helped either. But I guess they were worried about my reaction on them asking me to show them the wounds. I don't know whether I felt good about it or not but having been home was a good feeling altogether.

CHAPTER 11

I was no doubt feeling a little stable may be or I don't know what term I could actually use to describe the current situation. May be I could say I was just sailing through but my concentration power was bad even now. I could hardly afford to submit my assignments and the exams were near. I was worried about how would I give my exams when I could barely remember the previous line when I moved on to the next one. How am I going to take the exams in this state?

The next day I went to meet Charu ma'am and told her about my fear and explained to her the same.

"Do you still miss him?" She asked me outright.

"Of course I do" I said without even thinking for a minute.

"And do you still expect him to come back?"

"I know he will not. If he didn't come all these years how can I expect him to come now?"

"That's what you think, but what do you actually do? Think and answer to this" She said, asking me to think before I answered. But I didn't have to think much.

"Alright so I do know that he is not going to come back and it will be stupid of me to still think after whatever happened that he will come back, but the fact is that a part of me still does. Even today when I go home and am on the mall road my eyes look for him. I am worried what if I see him how will I be?"

"What bothers you? How will you be? Or is it the want to see him once?" she just hit the nail on the head.

"No it's just the fear of what my reaction would be on seeing him considering the situation am in now." I tried to convince her.

"Whom are you trying to convince dear, me or yourself?" And I laughed. I was caught.

"Yes, even today I wait for him to come back; just one glimpse of his is what I look forward to when I'm in Shimla. I don't know why. I know it's not the right thing but I still do, what do I do?"

Ma'am had this faint smile on her face and what she said next was something I wanted to hear but did now expect her to say it at all;

"Call him and talk to him then."

I looked at her as if she had just told me Akhil was outside waiting for me.

"Look if talking to him is what it takes for you to get slightly stable and be able to give your exams, go ahead and talk to him, but just be careful."

Now that was the entire problem you see 'be careful'. Be careful of what? Falling in love with him? Giving rise to hope again? Well he would do that again.

"Only if you are sure that this time you will not let him give you hopes of coming back and even if he does you will not take them seriously only then go ahead and talk to him." She said.

"Are you sure I should talk to him. I mean after all this and whatever happened in December should I really go and talk to him.?" I really wanted to but at the same time I was scared if I was doing the right thing or not.

"Yes" She looked at me confidently and blinked her eyes in assurance.

That day I left her cabin with a confused state of mind. On one hand she had asked me to do something I had been convincing myself not to do for so long and yet giving me terms and conditions to follow. I thought a lot about it that day or I could say all I thought of that day was this. Should I talk to him or should I not. I kept contemplating. I knew asking mom was not even an option, there was no way she would give consent to this in fact she will not let me talk to him at all. I spoke to Abhi even he said I should.

I sat down on my bed, took a deep breath typed his name and dialled his number.

"Hello" He said.

"Hi, Akhil how are you?" I asked.

"Hello" He said again trying to reconfirm if what he thought he heard was actually what he heard.

"Ya goel, can you hear me?"

"Aditi, is that you?"

"Yaa, are you ok? What happened?"

"It's now that you're calling? Couldn't you call earlier? What took you so long to call?"

"C'mon man, if I dint call neither did you, moreover you were the one to cut me off remember."

"Ya I remember, but you know na how am I."

"Yes I do but you could have called all this while, so much of ego?"

"Not ego yar."

"Then what? If you were missing me so much and so eager to talk why didn't you call?"

"Aditi, your mom asked me not to."

"Hmmm" I knew mom could have done that this time considering how ugly things had got last time.

"Acha sun, I'm outside right now, I'll just reach home and call you back. Ok?"

"Haha, this is just another excuse you're making to not talk, don't you think I know you way too well for this." I laughed.

"No ya, I will seriously call, you have no clue how much I have missed you, I just want to talk to you in peace, so just give some time to get back home and I will surely call you back." He said in a highly assuring tone.

"Cool, I'll be waiting" I said.

"Don't worry I will call."

The call disconnected, somehow I was not convinced that he would call back, so I just kept the phone aside happy with the feeling of having spoken to him after so long and to know that he missed me. Whether he calls or not one thing I was sure of and was very evident in the way he spoke was that he was actually very happy to talk to me and had missed me too. I just waited all evening for his call, time just flew by and I couldn't believe my eyes when the phone rang and I saw his number flashing on the screen. He was right that even he had been dying to talk to me. It was just the place and the time that was not appropriate when I called. That night we spoke for god knows how long, we just went on and on. Our talks didn't seem to be ending. We had so much to tell and share. I told him everything I had been going through and the state I was in. He too told me how he felt something was incomplete and how much he missed me. And the first thing I did after I kept his call was called up Roshni ma'am and told her everything.

"You sound so happy baby" she said.

"Yesssss, I am... I spoke to him after 4 months and knowing that he too missed me, I'm just so happy."

"I'm happy for you babes, but please be careful." She said.

My exams went off smoothly and I did pretty well I guess. I think it was the peace of mind his presence gave me that gave me comfort and everything passed away smoothly.

The semester got over and I was interning in Noida. It was just one the casual days when we were speaking over the phone;

"You know what goel I have started accepting and coming in terms with the fact that we can never be together." I just told him while we were talking about how I was doing health wise.

"Why do you have to think like that babe? It's a long life. You never know what would happen tomorrow" Now this statement left me baffled.

Are there still chances of him coming back? Am I giving up too soon? Should I still wait? Is he indicating that we will be together? What should I be interpreting of what he just said? He just said you never know we could be together in the future. Does this mean there is still hope and that the entire wait for all these years will have a good end?

Why does he do this over and over again? Just when I start accepting the reality and get in terms with it he says or does something taking me back to the state of hope and wait. His words kept playing with my mind for days together. I was just unable to brush those thoughts away. Mom could sense there was something wrong but I could not tell her that I had been talking to goel. I called up Charu ma'am and told her about the conversation and how it had been killing and disturbing me. She suggested that I talk to Akhil clearly about it and I too thought it would be the right thing to do and so I decided to call him.

"Wsup goel?" I asked him as soon he answered the call.

"Goel I wanted to talk to you about something that has been bothering me for quite some time now."

"Ya, tell me. Are you ok? Is everything fine?" He asked with concern.

"Not really, yar goel you remember that day when I said I am getting into terms with reality."

"Yup I remember."

"And do you remember what your answer to it was?" I asked.

"What?"

"You said I shouldn't think negative, you never know we could be together in the future. Did you really mean that Akhil?"

"Yar we are again getting into that old thing."

"No goel we are not I just want to know did you mean what you said that day, that's it."

"Aditi, no one knows what the future has in store for us."

"I know that Akhil, no one knows what will happen tomorrow all I'm asking you is did you mean it when you said we could be together?"

"I don't know ya."

"What is this akhil, what do you not know, I mean just when I am getting into terms with we not being together you... anyways chuck it. Temme something else?" We diverted from the topic but I was unable to get my mind off the conversation we just had and so I decided to end our talk that day.

I get it that you don't love me; it's my problem that I do. But what is with all these false hopes you keep giving me. You do things people do for their loved ones; you say things like this and then expect me to be cool with it. Don't you see what you're doing to me? I was unable to breathe. And this time it was for real that I was unable to breathe. I took a shower but that did not help. I was struggling to breathe and then what I did next was something not new to me but an indication that things were out of hand now. I harmed myself again and this time worse than before. The cuts were more and deeper but after that I could breathe. It was clear by now that what I was going through where panic attacks and now a counsellor alone could not help me. I called mom and told her the exact situation and she asked me to get the internship certificate for less days and get back home and I did so.

CHAPTER 12

This time when I was going home, bhai would also be there and it was holiday time. I was looking forward for a good time but at the same time I had to convince mom and dad that I was seriously ill and it was high time we went to the doctor. One good thing was that bhai was there. Even though I was not sure he knew the exact situation but once he would know, no one else can handle me better than him. I reached early in the morning at around 5 and slept off for a while. My wounds where fresh and would pain a lot. There was no medication I had used instead just tied crabe bandage around it so that people could not see it. As soon as mom left after tucking me in the bed I took off the bandage and slept. I'm sure when she came to check on me she did see blood on the bandage but didn't ask me any questions. She knew it would be very difficult for me to handle a situation of showing her the wound myself and so she didn't ask me to show it to her either. She gave me time to eventually on my own show it to her as it would definitely need bandage and care.

After I woke up bhai and me where just randomly playing and were just our normal selves when he unknowingly held my wrist tightly exactly where the cuts were. I screamed and started crying. He didn't have any clue about what happened, he thought it was just another tantrum to free myself from his grip unless mom saw me actually crying and running out of breath and asked bhai to leave my wrist at once. As soon as he released my hand I ran to my room shut the door and cried for a bit, calmed myself and lay down in the bed. Mom came in after a while and asked me if I was ok? I was still crying but assured her that I will be fine she asked me if I wanted her to put medicine or have I already done that. I just nodded my head.

"Someday I will see them, they need care at the moment, but I will not force you. Only when you are ready for it."

"Ok. "I struck my hand out and covered my face. She put some medicine and asked me to sleep for a while and come out when I felt like. I just kept lying down. I couldn't sleep but didn't have the strength to get out of bed. Bhai came in after an hour or so.

"I'm sorry di, I didn't know."

"It's ok bhaiya, you didn't do it purposely, I'm not mad at you" I smiled.

"If that's the case, shut up and get out of the bed."

If bhai asks me, even if I have broken legs I would run. I got out of bed and we started off again with our masti. It was a Sunday so we kept doing stuff with dad and beating him which is till date our favourite way of showing our love. It's our family thing you see. And in between our conversations mom assured me that we will be going to see the doctor soon. I was relieved.

The very next day mom, dad and bhai accompanied me to a doctor; she was a neurologist. Being a small town Shimla did not have too many options for good doctors. And fearing what if people found out we decided to visit this doctor who practices privately and was a neurologist. On examining she ruled out that I had reached a state where she could no longer do anything to help me and only a psychiatrist could give me proper medication and help me deal with this. On request and telling her that I get back to Jaipur only after a month and that I needed at least something to help me she put me on medication.

I was relaxed that at least we have taken the first step on the road to recovery. I knew it is going to be difficult because dealing with those medicines and getting the body used to them is a difficult task but I was determined to do that. Only two days after starting the medication. My body started to react to it. My body would go numb, hands would shiver, teeth kept clattering and I would remain disoriented most of the time, but thank god I was at home, with family they knew all this would happen and took extra care. We went for a vacation and it was during that time the medicines set in completely but the holiday made the entire process a little easier.

It was time for me to leave for Jaipur to get back to college. Bhai was to leave for college 10 days later and we decided that mom and dad will come with him to Jaipur and that is when we will visit a doctor in Jaipur. College started again. With medications on, I was fine sometimes except that the side effects kept poking in, but with Roshni ma'am around things was a lot simpler. I would see her face and would feel 100 times better. Mom and dad came to Jaipur and we had decided to see the psychiatrist at fortis and so we fixed an appointment and went to see him.

I never thought visiting a psychiatrist is going to be this hard. I kept telling myself that it's ok. It's a good thing that you know the problem and you are going to deal with it and get treated for it. Don't worry you'll be just fine. The waiting area outside his cabin just felt normal like at any other doctor's waiting hall, but as soon as you read the name with the title and specialisation written along with it your heart sinks. Damn, it's a psychiatrist. No I was not of the mindset that only people who are mad visit one but the fact that it was me who had to be here. Accepting the fact that someone like me whose confidence would be given as an example to people was waiting in a queue to be treated by a psychiatrist. I had fought for so long then why am I here now? Have I lost? Am I a looser? No I'm not. Just when I had a million thoughts running across my mind I held dad's arm tight and held on to him like this small child who is scared even with the thought of visiting a doctor. The attendant called out my name;

Patient name- "Aditi singh"

I was now a psychiatric patient. As we entered the doctor's cabin it seemed like this room with a soothing ambience with not too many things around and this man sitting with a computer on his side and a smile on his face.

"Hello"

"Hello doctor" we all greeted each other and sat down comfortably on the sofa's in the room.

"So tell me what happened?" He asked politely looking at the 3 of us one at a time. I just smiled and looked at him and then at mom and dad.

"It's ok, please feel comfortable and take your time and tell me" How could one be comfortable telling someone that you know what dude I think I'm going crazy and I harm myself. No one in the world can be comfortable with telling this to anyone. I was unable to find words to tell him what had happened and right then dad came to my rescue and said

"She hasn't been fine for a while now."

"Ok, and what has happened?" He looked at me and I just sat there quietly.

"You will have to talk to me dear, are you uncomfortable in front of your parents?" He asked me wondering if I was not saying anything because mom and dad where around.

"No no, not at all they know each and everything."

"Then what's the problem, it's just that I don't know what to say how to say it."

"Ok so let me make it easier for you, how about we start with the situation right now?"

"Yeah that seems better" and I tried to explain to him what exactly was the state and in the middle of my explanation he interrupted me and asked mom and dad to step out and said that he wanted to talk to me alone. Mom and dad went out and I kept sitting, he then asked me;

"Now do you want to go back a little?" And then I started.

"Well I fell in love with my best friend, he didn't. I waited he never came. He gave me hopes and took things

94

wrong; I don't know who's right who's wrong all I know is I'm in a mess now."

"And what do you mean by mess?"

"I mean, I'm no more what I used to be, my confidence level has gone down to zero, I hate being around people whereas at one point my friend's use to call me a social butterfly, but now crowd scares me. There was a time when I would not be scared to deliver speeches in front of 1000's of people but now I am too scared to even initiate a conversation, I have started harming myself, I get panic attacks, can't study, no dreams no aspirations. Don't know what I want to do with my career, I don't even know if I want one, no plans, in short career has been ruined. I just want to go back to shimla and be there. Just be and not do anything."

"You said panic attacks?"

"Yup."

"And what do you mean? As in what exactly happens when you have an attack?"

"I can hardly breathe; there is this choking feeling, a weird pain in the chest, a strangling feeling as if someone is trying to kill me, and there is this weird pain I can't explain."

"And do you harm yourself to get rid of this?"

"Exactly"

After this he called mom and dad in. And explained it to them that I was sick and had to start medication immediately, there were a few tests which had to be done to reconfirm the diagnosis. In the next two three hours the tests were completed and I was put on medication.

CHAPTER 13

      I had to come for a review every 15 days. The medication setting in was very difficult but mom, dad, bhai, Roshni ma'am, Abhi and Karan made it slightly easier.

  Karan was a college friend with whom I had lately got very close to. I would share everything with him. He was in Saudi but still he was always there for me and supported me and kept me going. Getting used to the medicines was very difficult, I could hardly eat, felt damn sleepy and drowsy, irritated all the time and threw up a lot. I was annoyed and irritated with the feeling.

  Panic attacks only got more ugly and worse. I was lying down in my bed on a Sunday afternoon when I got an attack I felt like a vegetable unable to move and breathe. I turned ice cold. Feet stiff like a rock, fists so tightly closed that no one could open them, gasping for air to breathe and teeth shut so tight that I could not speak at all. Tina di, my landlady came running and asked me what to do, but I was unable to direct her to my medicine which I was supposed to take if I got an attack. She called up mom and mom told her where the medicine would be. All she had to do was put the medicine under my tongue, open my fist and rub my feet. She had to struggle a lot to get me to open my mouth so that she could place the medicine under my tongue and after she did that she rubbed my feet and started to try to open my fist. After a while I was able to breather slightly better. It took almost an hour for me to calm down and the attack to settle down. I then spoke to mom and dad to assure them that I was fine, but it was very evident from the way I spoke which was slow soft and it took so much of effort to speak each word that there was no way I sounded fine. Dad asked me to rest and told me that mom is coming to Jaipur and will be there by morning. The next thing I remember is mom waking me up in the morning, as I lay lifeless in my bed with no energy to move or get up to greet her. She just kissed me, saw how my hand had blue marks as nails got dug in when I would close my fist tight during an attack and asked me sleep and rest and not get up. Neither did I have the energy to get up or move around nor did mom let me.

For the next few days mom stayed with me and took me around Jaipur to keep me happy. I was not forced to go to college but was convinced to go to maintain my attendance. I did go but not regular. The panic attacks were very frequent. On my next visit to the doctor mom came along and explained to him how ugly the attacks where getting and that the frequency was also bothering them.

"So are you going to college these days?" he asked. Just when mom was about to answer he said

"Aditi are you regularly going to college?"

"No."

"And why is that so? We had a deal right that you will go to college?"

"But I don't feel like. I hate it. There are so many people there. And if any teacher asks me anything I panic. I don't like it then, as people laugh."

"But your MBA will get affected right?"

"But I don't know what I want to do." Before I would panic again he asked me to calm down and scribbled something on my prescription and asked mom to take me to the counsellor for a session today itself.

The session was so annoying she just kept lecturing me how I should not let stuff affect my carrier. Blah blah. She just went on and on. By the time I came out I had a headache and told mom I just want to go back and sleep off. Counselling sessions where no more a relief like they use to be earlier with Charu ma'am. Instead whenever I went for one I always came back with a headache. At night while having medicines I realised the doctor had increased the medication to control the attacks. The next few days I felt weak but somehow a week passed by without an attack which for a change was a positive signal. It meant that the Medication was finally affecting me.

Mom was hesitant in leaving me alone and going back home. I assured her that I was fine and would anyways be coming home for rakhi in a week's time. Convinced that I will be able to manage myself at least for a week and considering the fact I have to learn how manage and not run away she left for home.

That week just flew and I went home for rakhi. That weekend went by really well. I had a very good time at home. And was happy. I was happy going back. On getting back I was excited to meet up with my cousin over the weekend and go shopping with all the money we had made during rakhi. We met on Saturday and for the whole day we shopped and ate, shopped and ate. Post that we were supposed to go to a relatives place to stay the night with them and nani too was there.

The evening went well. Nani wanted me to sing gurubani for everyone and do rehras sahib path which I gladly did. Later we all sat, had a chit chat session and slept off. Next morning my elder cousin was in a lazy mood and to cheer and wake him up I gave him a good head massage. I had to leave back for my pg that day as I had college the next day and I don't know why suddenly I had a very uncomfortable feeling and again didn't want to be with so many people. I was just suddenly disturbed and irritated. I thought it was another attack and its best that I go back. I was just lying down with everyone when I got an attack. Thankfully my cousins managed to hide it from the family and put me to bed. After a while when I felt slightly better I called for a cab and went back.

I was still in the post panic attack mode and was not feeling too good. I was having all negative thoughts possible and my mind was stuck in the conversation between me and Akhil which we had that day regarding we being together in the future. I kept talking to Karan to avoid another attack and to keep calm. I reached home and spoke to my landlady for a while and then as I was very tired and upset at the same time went up to my room.

After my attacks having taken a toll I was strictly told never to lock my room so that in case of an attack my flatmate or my landlords could come in. So I just changed and unlocked the door and decided to lie down for a while before having dinner, having medicines and going off to sleep. I felt extremely uneasy. I didn't know what was wrong but something was not fine. The weird creepy feeling was annoying me. I tried crying but couldn't, called Abhi to talk to him but couldn't talk much. I was just restlessly turning and tossing and became completely numb. While writing a text to a few friends in a state when I didn't have any clue what I was writing I just got up grabbed every possible liquid that got my way poured it in a glass sat down on my bed took out the medicines I was supposed to have and had them with a glass full of all sought of liquids from perfumes to nail polish removers to mortein to orange juice and sent that message to I don't remember who all.

Just when I finished the glass my roommate came in casually and asked me if I was fine as Karan on receiving my text called her up to go and stop me. She had not even finished saying what she wanted to when di came running from downstairs and started screaming, "she has consumed something." While she was saying this I fell down and they held me.

I was in a very weird state. I knew what was happening around. Even though my eyes were closed I could hear what was happening around me. I knew they constantly asked me to wake up but I just couldn't. I couldn't move or respond. They slapped me, pinched and threw water. But I just lay there. I passed out. The only thing I remember is that I was sitting on a chair in the middle of the road waiting for I don't know who and what to take me to the hospital just when nanu and nani came in their car and rushed me to the hospital. I saw Priya standing there crying and shouting my name and screaming and asking me to get up. I guess I had sent her the message I had typed. I was taken inside and on checking my pulse before I passed out I was taken into the emergency room. I passed out again.

The next I remember is I woke on the emergency table in the operation theatre with doctors and nurses all around me pinching and slapping me, poking me with needles and saying something I have no clue about... I just opened my eyes and saw this doctor inserting a long tube from my nose through my throat into the stomach. I could see fluid coming out of the tube and knew what was happening. They kept putting in some fluid and then pressing my stomach and lower abdomen and flushing it out. They continued doing this for half an hour or so after which they asked me to speak.

"What is your name?" I heard this rude voice asking me.

"Aditi" I said and burst out in tears.

"Why are you crying?" She asked me.

"I don't want to die." I said.

"Then why did you do this?" She asked scolding me.

"I don't knowww... I'm sick... I don't want to die" I just kept saying this until one of the doctors saw medicines coming out in the pipe. He shook me and asked what have you consumed." I told him whatever I remembered from the liquid I drank.

"Tell us the truth. You have taken some pills also, right?. Don't lie. We will not be able to save you if you don't tell us the truth" He shouted.

"I am on medication for depression from the past 6 months. I'm sick. Please don't scold me."

There was complete silence in the room after I shouted this out. I guess now they knew they were not dealing with a person who just suddenly thought that she could not deal with life and decided to die. They knew now that I was sick for which I was on medication and that whatever just happened, I was probably not even mentally in my senses when all this happened and the only way to deal with such a patient was with patience. I turned my head away from the lights and saw mami g standing at door crying and shouted please let me meet mami g please let me see my cousin but they just wouldn't let me. It was only when all the doctors left; the attendant let both of them in for 2 minutes when they just loved me with tears running down their cheeks. "Don't worry we all are with you and you will be fine."

After god knows how long I was transferred to the ICU with all the tubes and what not. I remember my cousin instructing everyone not to overreact on seeing me. I just passed all of them and held on to my cousins hand with all the little strength I had and kept looking at him with eyes that almost shut down. On settling me in the ICU he said;

"Baby, you could have told me just once that you were so worried and in trouble, anyways, just get well soon now, you have to give me a head massage again, you can't escape that." and he had tears in his eyes.

I just blinked my eyes and asked him for my phone which he refused to give and told me that mom and dad have already left. He was then asked to leave as the doctors had to fix in a few more machines and monitor me. They didn't let me sleep that night. I cried in pain. Neither did they take the tube out nor did they give me a painkiller to let me sleep and in no time my head was splitting into two. It was only after hours together of screaming in pain did the doctor give me a mild painkiller to make the pain bearable. The pain I went through that night is not something I can explain.

At around 4 in the morning mom and dad arrived and they where let in one by one. Dad came in and on seeing him I just turned my face away because I didn't know how to face him or what to say;

"Look at me princess. Look daddy is here" He said crying.

I turned and looked at him and cried.

"I'm sorry dad, I'm a really bad daughter."

"No baby, you're the best, just don't worry daddy will take you home now and you will be completely fine see mommy is waiting outside." He pointed at the ICU window and I waved at her weakly and the attendant let her in. She just kissed me and said." Don't worry you'll be fine"

The attendant let mom sit with me and she put me off to sleep. Sometime later the doctor came and checked on me and said I was out of danger but we will have to keep the tubes for a few more hours. I was in pain and mom could see it so she again put me off to sleep and left. It was around 9 when mom, dad and nani came in and woke me up. Dad hugged me and said; "All your stuff is packed and daddy is taking princess home and now you will be fine."

The doctor came in and finally after examining me took out the tubes and sent me for a couple of test. After a few hours he saw the reports and said I was fine and when dad told him that we want to take her to Shimla and that the further treatment would be done there, he gave his consent. I was given a shower and out from the hospital straight into the car and I left everything behind and went home.

Roshni ma'am had been in constant touch with mom and dad and once I was a little stable, I spoke to her for a minute to assure her I was fine. As I was lying on the icu bed and saw priya, mom, dad, cousins and family. Somewhere when mom and dad arrived my eyes did look out hoping even Akhil would have come but never dared to ask mom or dad. But mom while feeding me dinner said;

"I called him up to tell him what had happened; I saw how you looked for him. Darling he has not come. On finding this out, all he said was – "What's my fault in it, there's nothing I can do."

I heard these lines and just quietly sat back in the car and we drove off.

I reached home and days passed by. I was getting better but was always quiet and would cry with stomach pain very often. I could barely eat or digest anything.

He did not rush to Jaipur with mom and dad, fine, he said it's not my fault, accepted but he never bothered to even find out how I was. Whether I survived the night or died. He just never asked or tried to find out. Now this hurts. It hurts a lot. A person whom I loved so much, a person who gave me false hope but I still never blamed him, the person because of who's hopes I am in the situation I am in but I don't blame him for that, that very person has not even made the effort to find out whether I'm dead or alive. I know he doesn't love me but even for humanity sake he just did not call or come home. Not that I wanted him to come say I love you, but at least as a friend, as an acquaintance or just as a human being he could have at least made a courtesy call.

It was a very difficult time for me and even more for my family. Not only was I in a bad shape physically but also recovering very slowly mentally. Even though slow but I was and on my road to recovery I had an encounter with Akhil. I was frozen on seeing him coming from the front for a moment I thought maybe he stops and talks but instead he just hung his head down and passed by. I broke down but decided not to leave because his head was hung in shame for not being human enough and not mine. I went home. it was a difficult night for all of us but with the next morning came a decision that this is it. Now he will live with his head hung down and with the regret for having done what he did and not me. God has given me a new life and mom dad and bhai are with me. I will start afresh.

THE END

I loved him but he didn't, He said we are friends and I was happy with it.

He said we can never be together but he can't even live without me, I was still ok with it.

He loved someone else I supported him because we were best friends.

He kept going and coming back I dealt with it.

Everyone except him thought he loved me, I lived with it.

I lost hopes and fell, he still gave me hopes of being together even after all the years when he never came back I didn't stop loving him.

I still said that even if he realizes today I will go back to him

I almost died and he just didn't care. No I'm not ok with this. Not because you didn't find out how your friend was, but because you were not human enough to do so and this time "It's over... forever and it's over for good"

It's time for me to be reborn again. I had lost myself to your love and I will discover the new me falling out of love. I had given up all battles in life as I was so busy trying to win you but now I will win and get back the life I lost. I loved you so much that I forgot all my dreams; I will now love mine and my parent's dreams and make the world love and remember me.

EPILOGUE

Two years later...

Love comes; either stays with you and makes you or leaves you and ruins you, but you stay, collect all the broken pieces and walk again.

It is 7 am and Aditi is getting ready for a press conference, to address the media regarding the success of her organisation. An organisation that helps people to deal with depression and bipolar disorder. The organisation today is a pioneer in the field of mental health. It has not been an easy way up here. Fighting each day with past and its impact on her life had been a battle she had to fight every single day.

What made you get into this line?

"I followed my heart, I loved and lost but what I lost to was not the man I loved but the disease and I don't want anyone else to lose to it. Because when you lose love you loose hope, faith and life but at the end of the day you can get up and find more love as there is plenty of it but if you lose yourself the battle is lost. And we as humans don't decide when we could die and living a lost battle is not worth it."

Do you regret loving?

No I don't, but I regret loving someone else more than my own self.

Don't you fear what will the society say as you come out in the open about your personal life while working for the organization?

That's the motive of my organisation to heal within the society and not by running away from it. And loving is no crime neither is falling sick. No one falls sick by choice.

Do you also believe in the "True love happens only once" phenomena?

No

"When I lost him I lost a battle as I lost the one I loved, but when he lost me he lost a war because I can love someone else the way I loved him, but he will never be loved the way I loved him."

THE END